At every step, however, they're thwarted by:

WINTERPOLE, a global bureaucratic rule maker.

Their goal?
  To be an icicle in the side of progress.

How they do it?
  Governing by permission slip.

VESUVIA PIFFLE, a rival eleven-year-old continent-creator.

Her job?
  Super-secret CEO of the villainous Condo Corp.

Her obsession?
  All things pink and plastic.

"Wait a minute, Evie. Winterpole bylaws clearly state that they have jurisdiction over everything on all *seven* continents. But if we transform trash island, it would be big enough to be called a new continent. The Eighth Continent."

"You mean Winterpole wouldn't be able to tell us what to do? Ooooh, Rick! This is cool. This is cool-plus. We have to do this."

MATT LONDON

razOr
bill

An Imprint of Penguin Group (USA), LLC

For my family

razOr bill

A division of Penguin Young Readers Group
Published by the Penguin Group
Penguin Group (USA) LLC
345 Hudson Street
New York, New York 10014

USA / Canada / UK / Ireland / Australia / New Zealand
India / South Africa / China
Penguin.com
A Penguin Random House Company

ISBN: 978-1-59514-754-7

CIP data is available

Printed in the United States of America

1 3 5 7 9 10 8 6 4 2

"IF YOU KIDS DON'T KNOCK IT OFF, I'M GOING TO TURN THIS TREE AROUND AND GO HOME!"

At her father's command, Evie Lane removed the two fingers she had curled into her brother's nostrils. "But, Dad! We're so close to the Buhana Jungle I can hear the bird-songs! I can smell the mangoes!"

Her brother, Rick, who at eleven was one year older than Evie and never let her forget it, released the grip he had on a lock of her wavy dark hair. "Mangoes aren't indigenous to the Buhana Jungle. Everyone with a hundred sixty IQ knows that."

Evie leaned back in her wood-carved cockpit chair and made a long, drawn-out snorting sound, like a snore. "*Zszszszszsog!* If only you used that big brain of yours for something other than shooting laser beams at space marines in your video games."

Rick adjusted the glasses on his blushing face. "Studies show video games improve spatial reasoning and hand-eye coordination."

"Coordinate your way to the evac room. We land in the Buhana Jungle in t-minus real soon." Their father did not look away from the main viewport of the *Roost*'s cockpit as he spoke.

"Nerds first," Evie said, offering Rick the chance to lead the way.

"Jerks second," Rick retorted, racing toward the back of the Lane family's personal hovership. He ducked under the hollow branches that piped water and fuel throughout the aircraft.

The *Roost* was unlike any flying machine the world had ever seen. It was carved from a giant sequoia named King Sargon that had fallen victim to a lightning strike in Yosemite National Park. Dad had discovered the great fallen tree while in the region rejuvenating bald eagle habitats. He took the remains back home to Switzerland, where he carved rooms and passageways through the trunk of the broken titan. Two custom repulsor engines had been grafted to its roots, which allowed the tree to fly at supersonic speeds.

In fourteen seconds (a new record) Evie and Rick reached the evac room, a large compartment where the exit ramp deployed.

Standing in the corner of the room was their robot teacher, 2-Tor, a seven-foot-tall mechanical crow. 2-Tor's eyes glowed with life. Colors swirled on the video screen in his belly.

The birdbot stepped forward, flapping his chromium wings and cocking his head from side to side. When he spoke, his digitized voice sounded faintly British. "Aha! So you have deigned to grace me with your presences at last. Miss Evelyn, you are late for your algebra practice test."

"Sorry, 2-Tor," Evie said with an innocent smirk. "Duty calls!"

2-Tor hooted like an owl that had swallowed a kazoo. "If you continue to neglect your studies, Miss Evelyn, you will flunk your math exam . . . again! Mister Richard has never flunked anything in his life!"

Evie glared at Rick sourly. 2-Tor was always on her case. He never lectured Rick. Sometimes Evie suspected that her brother must have hacked into 2-Tor's software and changed his programming so that 2-Tor would let him do whatever he wanted.

In this case, however, Rick came to her defense. "Difficult as it is to believe, 2-Tor, it isn't Evie's fault this time. Dad has us on another one of his ridiculous missions to 'save an innocent bird from the evils of trash.'"

That was putting it lightly. In recent years, many of the earth's most beautiful regions had been turned into dumping grounds. Deserts were doused in trash. Caves were clogged. Forests were overflowing! The Buhana Jungle was no exception. It was a festering wound poisoning the earth, jammed full of junk no one wanted anymore.

Evie's dad sauntered into the room dressed like a goofy astronaut. His pointed nose and pouf of auburn hair made it look like the sun was rising behind his head. He zipped up his brown flight suit. "I've set the *Roost* to autopilot. Now remember, kids, the Buhana Jungle is the only habitat of the rare bird known as the Buhana of Paradise. If we don't rescue this specimen, the whole species could be wiped out."

Evie fidgeted as the Buhana Jungle grew large in the *Roost*'s portholes. The toxic storage site in this tropical paradise belonged to the Condo Corporation, a real estate and construction company that was owned by the father of the most popular girl at Evie's school, Vesuvia Piffle. She was Empress of the Academy, and if you wanted to be anybody at the International School for Exceptional Students, you needed Vesuvia's approval. Without it, you were nothing, a smear of mustard on the cafeteria floor that the janitor would mop up at the end of fifth period.

If Vesuvia found out that Evie's family was raiding Condo Corp property, there was no telling what the platinum-blond monster would do. Maybe Vesuvia would hire a robo-shop quartet to follow Evie around school, and everywhere she went the robots would sing about what a poorly dressed and smelly loser she was. Then only Rick would hang out with her . . . and no one hung out with Rick.

"Everybody ready?" Evie's father grinned like he had woken up to discover he had grown wings overnight. "Suits on! Grab your mouthmasks! Fresh water and cleaning supplies . . . check! Let's go get that bird."

Evie glanced out the window again at the ever-approaching jungle. "Dad, it looks like we're coming in too fast."

"Never fear, daughter dear! Compared to the *Roost*'s top speed, we will be landing at a snail's pace!"

Compared to the *Roost*'s top speed, a snail's pace meant they landed at approximately a zillion miles an hour. Old car tires, broken logging equipment, and other trash-dump projectiles went flying as the rocket-powered tree roared across the jungle, carving a canyon out of the littered landscape.

The Lane family hopped off the exit ramp and sank up to their waists in trash-filled mud. Evie struggled to pull her arms free of the sludge.

"Trash." Dad retched, attaching a white respirator to his nose and mouth. "There is nothing I despise more than poorly discarded unsanitary waste products."

Evie gagged. "Ugh! It smells like lasagna made with old socks."

"Yech!" Rick added. "It smells like a toilet brush on an all-asparagus diet!"

Dad fanned away a swarm of flies. "I invented those deodorizing mouthmasks to block out unwanted odors and unwanted complaints! It does me no good if you don't wear them."

Evie fitted the mouthmask over her face and was surprised at how well it concealed the overwhelming stench. After so many missions with her dad around the world, swimming neck-deep in garbage and saving animals from damaged habitats, she was glad to have something to block out the nauseating smell. She turned to tell Dad that his latest invention was totally awesome, but he was already several feet ahead of her, cutting a path through the mud.

The Buhana Jungle looked almost as Evie had imagined

it, with densely packed trees, mud, tangled roots, and a grand canopy of leaves high overhead. Wrecked chainsaw trucks and demolition vehicles were upturned everywhere. Discarded power cables hung like snakes from the trees, and billowing plastic bags suffocated many branches.

In the distance, a kapok tree emerged from the heaps of scrap metal, empty food containers, and bulging trash bags. This must have been where Condo Corp's deforestation crews dumped their waste when they weren't chopping down hundred-year-old trees to make room for one of the company's signature properties. A massive billboard hanging from a tree read: "Take a swing at all eighteen stories of Condo Corp's new Vertical Golf Course!" Evie shook her head. The corporation's willingness to destroy the environment for the sake of something pointless never ceased to amaze.

When Evie and Rick reached the kapok tree, Dad was already shimmying up the trunk. He tugged on a branch and cooed softly. "Hey there, little fella. It's okay. No one's going to hurt you."

"Did you find the bird?!" Evie squinted to see what or whom her dad was talking to.

"Shh!" Rick nudged her. "You're gonna scare it away."

Evie didn't want to frighten the bird, but she couldn't help hurrying. She had a bad feeling about trespassing on Condo Corp property.

Rick must have felt the same way, because as their father hopped out of the tree, he said, "Dad, we really shouldn't be here. We're breaking the rules. You're going to get caught again, and Mom isn't going to like that."

"But, Rick, we're saving the planet! What is there to complain about?"

Rick flapped his arms like a grumpy eagle, spattering the ground with trash and mud. "Come on! I swore on my Game Zinger that I wouldn't let you get caught again."

"Your mother will understand that I am doing this for the greater good . . . I hope." Dad opened his hands, revealing the limp shape of the Buhana of Paradise. Its sapphire-and-ruby feathers were so soiled with grime that it looked like it was covered in belly button lint. The remains of a plastic sandwich bag were knotted around its feet.

"Aww, poor thing!" Evie said.

"But, hey, we found him!" Dad said.

"Yeah, we did!" Rick cheered.

"Go Team Lane!" Evie gave Rick a high five, for the moment forgetting their differences. One thing they could agree on was that saving an injured bird was a good thing.

Dad watched the exchange between the kids, grinning. Then he jumped back to work. "Evie, help me with the scissors. Rick, did you bring the wash bucket?"

Rick slid the scroll of super plastic out of its carrying tube. He handed it to his father. With a flick of his wrist, Dad unrolled the flat plastic and popped it into the correct wash-bucket shape.

Just as Evie cut the bird free of its bonds with her scissors, the hum of a hover engine filled the air. "Uh, what's that?" Dread filled Evie's voice.

A floating petunia came down through the leafy canopy, its bright plastic petals spiraling like helicopter blades. The pink flying machine moved toward them, dodging branches, sirens blaring. Evie's heart sank.

The pink flowercopter came down to eye level, where they could see its robotic interface, a number of multi-jointed grasping arms, and a video screen with a face on it. But not just any face: the face of Evie's classmate, Vesuvia Piffle.

She spoke with a sharp, squeaky voice, like a cross between a cartoon princess and a homicidal maniac. "Intruders! This wilderness preserve has been claimed by the Condo Corporation as a waste dumping ground. You are trespassing on private property! Ha! Daddy will be so proud when he sees that all by myself I caught three thieving— wait. Evie?"

Evie tried to hide her face from the rotating camera on top of the video monitor.

"Evie Lane, it *is* you! I'd recognize that hideous taste in clothing anywhere. *You're* the one trespassing? *You're* the one stealing from Daddy's company?!"

Evie turned to her father for help, but he was preoccupied with washing the bird. "Vesuvia, I can explain."

"I bet you can!" Vesuvia sneered. "You can explain to the other girls at school why you're the biggest loser ever."

"Please," Evie begged. "Give me another chance. We're just trying to save the bird. What are you going to do?"

Vesuvia's tone turned angelic. "Oh me? Nothing."

"Really?!" Evie exclaimed. "Oh, thank you. I'm so sorry. I'll never—"

Vesuvia began to cackle, the sound drowning out Evie's frantic apology. "That's nice. Tell it to Winterpole. Something tells me they won't be as forgiving." The flower-copter turned to the sky, where several sleek hoverships burst through the canopy in an explosion of leaves. "See you at school, thief!" echoed Vesuvia's voice.

Evie's stomach dropped.

Winterpole, the international police agency dedicated to making sure nothing ever changed, not even a little bit, had been an icicle in the Lane family's side as long as Evie could remember. If something existed on any of the seven continents, Winterpole had jurisdiction over it. The bureaucracy of the organization was so impenetrable that they rarely accomplished anything, and they always slowed down the innovations of her father, who genuinely cared about helping the environment. All Winterpole did was follow its mission statement of "Organization and Documentation of Natural Property," whatever that meant.

Fearful accusations filled Rick's eyes. "Dad, what's Winterpole doing here?"

"Well, you know how the Buhana Jungle is the last remaining habitat of the Buhana of Paradise?"

"Uh-huh." The kids shared a look. They knew how this story would end.

"So, unfortunately, in order to protect the species,

Winterpole created a law prohibiting anyone from removing a bird of its kind from its home."

Evie could not contain her offense. "Wait a sec. So you're saying that to protect the bird, Winterpole made a rule that you can't take it out of the habitat that's *killing* it?"

"Yes, that's exactly it." Dad shook his head. "Ridiculous, right? The operatives there just don't think; they issue statutes without regard to whether a particular environment is, say, a toxic dump. If I could just get in front of them, I'd—"

One of Rick's veins was bulging so much it looked like it was about to leap free and go for a jog.

"You okay there, son?" George asked.

"Dad, we know Winterpole is far from super effective, but what you're telling us is that in order to save this bird, you broke Winterpole bylaws, risked the integrity of Lane Industries, and endangered the lives of your children?"

"No!" Dad replied. "I haven't done all that." He tucked the bird into the front of his flight suit. "Okay, now I'm doing all that. Run! To the *Roost*."

They waded through the mud back to their enormous hovership, Rick nagging like their mother did the whole way. But Evie barely heard his complaints; the memory of Vesuvia Piffle's vile cackles still filled her ears. Evie would have to change her name and go to junior high in Finland. There was no telling what that perky pain would do.

2

RICK STOOD ON A BALCONY AT THE BACK OF THE ROOST, WATCHING THE BUHANA JUNGLE VANISH

beyond the horizon. A fierce breeze whipped at his freshly showered hair. The Pacific Ocean stretched out in every direction, an azure blanket. Two thousand feet below him, waves rose and fell like the belly of the Snorivore monster in *Animon Hunters*. He searched the sky for any sign of Winterpole hoverships that might be chasing them.

Amazingly, Dad seemed to have given the agency the slip once again.

Most people would feel cold and isolated when looking at such a vast, empty sight. For Rick, however, it was nothing special. He felt cold and isolated all the time. Sure, he went to a pretty cool school, with sushi bento boxes for lunch and a third period class in video game design, but he had zero friends. Zero. The boys were mean, the girls were gross, and his teacher had less personality than a robot (and with parents like Rick's, he knew a thing or two about robots).

Evie was the only person who was halfway nice to him, even when it meant the girls at school would tease her for acknowledging the existence of a kid who preferred study hall to recess. He loved her for that. Evie once started a food fight at the mall with a high school boy who'd made fun of Rick's interest in obscure video games. The look on the kid's face when Evie catapulted a two-gallon barrel of grape pudding at him was something Rick would never forget.

This happy memory faded as Rick, ever the focused perfectionist, brought himself back to the present. What bothered him the most was this trouble with his dad. Lane Industries had been developing cutting-edge technologies since the time of Rick's grandfather, the company's founder. He had encouraged George, a genius scientist in his own right, to focus his research on robotics, engineering, propulsion, construction, climatology, and other cool fields like that. After Rick's grandfather passed away, Dad continued the Lane family tradition, creating robots and hoverships that were now used all over the world, including—as they'd only just discovered—by Evie's nemesis, Vesuvia.

Recently, however, Rick's dad had been spending more time on little pet projects, like saving rare birds and building them new habitats with roller coasters and birdbaths the size of Olympic swimming pools. Rick wanted him to focus on the important stuff, like keeping Lane Industries a viable business and not risking the future of the company—and their family—by breaking Winterpole's never-ending list of rules.

2-Tor's metallic voice blatted out of the splintering

loudspeaker hanging over the door. "Richard! Your father would like to show you something important. Please report to the cockpit without delay."

Tardiness had been known to cause Rick to break out in hives, so he sprinted to the front of the *Roost*. The interior of the cockpit looked like a palatial living room, with fluffy carpets, leather sofas, a holographic display table, and a control console shaped like a pipe organ with ninety-seven various buttons and gauges. A sloped glass window stretched across the front wall.

Rick's father was sitting behind the flight stick, studying a few blips on the navigation monitor and letting his well-crafted hovership do most of the work. Evie sat in the copilot's chair, spinning in circles. Sometimes Rick didn't know how he and Evie were the same species, let alone brother and sister. That girl would rather scale the walls of their school with a grappling hook than sit inside and ace spelling bees. She was never happy in the moment, always looking for adventure. Meanwhile, Rick's own idea of adventure was swinging from vines in *Jungle Joust 2*, an awesome retro arcade game he had downloaded the week before. He was glad that the game gave him the opportunity to, as the advertisement for the game suggested, "live life on the wild side." He would never do something like that in real life. He might fall and break his neck.

"2-Tor told me it was urgent?" Rick said when neither his father nor his sister turned around to greet him. Still getting no response, he added, "I did a visual scan of the area. No sign of Winterpole hoverships anywhere. But that doesn't mean that they're not out there."

His father continued studying the display screens, ignoring Rick like he always did when he had one of his crazy ideas.

"Dad, I don't see why you insist on being Winterpole enemy number one. Is there some sort of prize? A coupon for fifty percent off birdseed?"

"Yeah, uh-huh." George finally looked up. "I want to show you my new project."

Rick breathed a sigh of thank-goodness. His father was actually involving him in Lane Industries' latest venture. The more Rick knew about the company, the better he would be at running the family business when he eventually took it over.

"What's the project, Dad?" Evie asked.

"Garbage!"

Garbage. That didn't surprise Rick at all. His father had made a fortune creating new engines, robots, and other incredible inventions, but his passion had always been for ridding the world of waste. Whether turning old landfills into public parks or recycling bottles and cans into motorcycles, Dad was always trying to make the grass greener, the ocean bluer, and the air clearer.

"What are we doing way out here, then?" Evie asked. "There's no garbage out here."

"Quite the contrary," Dad replied. "Take a look out the front window."

Rick wrenched his face in disgust as he peered down

14

at the water. There was so much trash it made the Buhana Jungle look like the wastebasket under his bathroom sink.

What appeared to be the world's largest collection of empty drink bottles covered the water. They bobbed on the waves, gray weathered plastic reflecting the sun's harsh rays. The labels that had not fallen off the bottles were faded white.

"Did a Pepsi shipping freighter sink?" Evie asked.

2-Tor wagged a metal feather at her. "Evelyn, you know quite well that is incorrect."

"Any ideas, Rick?" George asked.

Rick adjusted his glasses. "According to the *Roost*'s Global Positioning System, at the moment we are flying over what's known as the North Pacific Gyre. It's an area in the Pacific where a bunch of ocean currents swirl together in a kind of vortex. That must be what brought all this trash here. People litter, then the trash gets washed out to sea. The trash floats along with the currents until it ends up here. But, Dad, we really need to talk about Winterpole. What's Mom going to say when she finds out—"

His father interrupted, "Ocean currents! Exactly right, Rick. Well done!"

Evie scowled. "Give me a second and I could have come up with that answer too."

In the distance, what looked like a big island came into view. As the hovership got closer, Rick saw that it was a giant mountain of trash. It was so enormous he couldn't see the ends of it. It stretched to infinity in three directions. Rolling hills of milk jugs, soda cans, car tires, and shopping bags. Vast plains of yogurt cups and potato chip cans, dotted with little green baskets that used to house strawberries and crumpled plastic sheets peeled off the back of fruit roll-ups.

There were a million specks of junk. Stretched and worn and waterlogged, the expanse of trash created a surface that looked almost dense enough to walk on.

"Oh, I've heard about this!" Evie said. "The Great Pacific Garbage Patch."

Rick had heard about it too—all the garbage in the North Pacific Gyre sticking together to create one immense island in the middle of the ocean. "Is it really the size of Texas?" he asked.

His father chortled. "Oh-ho, no. It's nothing like that. Well, sort of. This here, what most people consider the garbage patch, is actually just a tiny piece of it. It's not as large as Texas. More like . . . Rhode Island. But we've scooped up trash from all over the oceans and transported it here. Most of the garbage patch, which is *twice* the size of Texas, is more like a filmy soup of chemicals with little bits of weathered plastic floating in it. Smells awful!" He pinched his nose for effect.

"Are you trying to clean up the garbage patch?" Evie asked.

Hearing her question, Rick knew that this couldn't quite be it. If it was, then why would his father have *brought* additional trash here instead of just disposing of the trash that already existed?

Sure enough, Dad replied, "Not exactly! Look over there!" He pointed out the window at what appeared to be a trio of enormous metal elephants floating on the water. Each machine was so big that just one of them could easily fill Rick's school gymnasium. All stood rigidly at attention, gray legs and trunks locked straight. As the machines moved over the surface of the water, they gobbled up the trash in their way, depositing blocks of plastic as they passed by.

"What are those things?" Rick asked, his eyes almost as wide as his glasses.

"Those are my garbage chompers," his father said. "Aren't they cute?"

Evie wrinkled her nose at the sight of the garbage-guzzling elephant bots. She patted Dad's shoulder. "*Cute* is not the word I would use, but sure, Dad. Sure."

"Have I ever told you my dreams of island building?" their father asked.

"A society on the sea?" Rick winked at Evie.

"Lane Industries' Ocean Empire!" Evie said in her best imitation of her exuberant father.

Rick rolled his eyes. "Only about two billion times."

"Children!" 2-Tor interrupted. "It's time for a quiz. Mathematics. What is two billion in scientific notations?"

Rick didn't miss a beat. "Two times ten to the ninth power."

Evie stuck her tongue out at him. Rick made a mental note to design a mechanical grasping claw that could pinch her whenever she did that.

"Excellent, 2-Tor! Excellent!" George exclaimed, sitting up straight and smug. 2-Tor's job was to keep Rick's and Evie's minds sharp with surprise quizzes when they missed school on their adventures. Dad looked quite pleased with the way the educational birdbot was working, but he didn't let his satisfaction with his invention distract him from the mission at hand. "Now, pay attention, children," he continued. "This trash-gobbling venture is my latest attempt at island building. Just think, with the garbage processed into plastic blocks, we can use the pieces as building materials to construct a land-mass, right here in the middle of the Pacific Ocean. Then all the world's birds will have a safe place to live, free of toxic, glow-in-the-dark fish and plastic booby traps."

Something large passed in front of the sun, casting Rick, his father, and his sister into shadow. Rick looked up to see two hoverships fly overhead. "Winterpole! I knew this would happen!"

"Incoming message," Evie said, reading off the com-municator screen. "'George Lane! We are locked on to your vessel. Attempts to escape will prove fuh-tilly.'"

"It says *futile*," Rick groaned.

The Lanes had no choice but to set the *Roost* to hover mode and listen to Winterpole's demands. George pushed away from the console and headed out of the cockpit. "Come on. Let's go see what they want."

Rick followed Evie and their dad through the winding, wooden passageways and returned to the balcony over-looking the garbage patch.

The Winterpole hoverships looped around the *Roost*, pulling up in front of the Lanes' hovership. A sliding door on the side of the lead ship opened, revealing a middle-aged man in a trim gray suit. His eyes were the color of faded jeans, and he wore a fedora that covered his hair, save for his graying sideburns.

"George Lane!" the man shouted over the wind and the roaring engines. "I have caught you at last."

"Who are you?" George asked.

The man looked offended. "What? It is I, Mister Snow."

"Sorry, the name doesn't ring any diamonds."

The offense on his face turned to annoyance. "I'm a penalty enforcer for Winterpole."

George continued to stare at him blankly.

"Mister Snow? We've met six or seven times."

George shrugged.

"Never mind!" snapped Mister Snow. "You are in violation of Winterpole Statutes 23-12, 41, A-76, and 31-B. Statute 31-B is kind of a big deal."

George snorted. "Your alphabet soup doesn't mean anything to me. What was my crime?"

"You removed a bird from its protected habitat."

Evie couldn't contain her fury. "But the bird couldn't live in the habitat anymore! He'd die there. We saved him! Why don't you go annoy the people who created the dumping ground?"

"Winterpole has rules against removing birds from protected habitats. There is no such rule against dumping waste on a protected habitat."

"Well there should be," Evie spat in disgust.

"Careful," Mister Snow replied. "There is a rule against suggesting new Winterpole rules."

While Evie screamed for a while about double standards

and justice, Rick wondered what his mother would say about Dad's latest run-in with Winterpole. Sometimes Rick thought his dad was the dumbest genius he had ever met. Rick never had trouble following the rules, but his dad was a different kettle of fishsticks. It was almost like he enjoyed behaving badly. The thought of acting that way made Rick sick from his nostrils to his knuckles.

Mister Snow continued. "The penalty board has evaluated your crimes and determined that the price you will pay is the immediate destruction of these machines. You will be placed under house arrest pending further case review."

Rick had to restrain Evie to keep her from leaping off the balcony and attacking Mister Snow. She shrieked, "You can't do this!"

"I'm just doing my job, miss. Your father is a known bird thief. He must be brought to justice."

"Bird? What bird? I don't see any bird around here, do you?" It was one of Evie's obvious ploys. Rick didn't know what she hoped to accomplish.

"*Wark!*"

The squawk made Rick stop short.

"*Waaaark!*"

Mister Snow made no effort to hide his smug expression. A colorful fan of feathers had burst out from the bottom of George Lane's shirt. The luminescent blue head of a Buhana of Paradise poked out the top and looked around.

"*Wark! Waaaaark!*"

Mister Snow had made his point. The hoverships rocketed

away from the *Roost*, heading toward the garbage chompers. Trapdoors opened in the canopies of the hoverships, and sledgehammers the size of city buses emerged.

"No!" Rick's father cringed. "I knew I never should have invented the flying hammer arm."

Without hesitation, the ships swung their hammers at the garbage chompers, smashing out the legs of the machines, breaking off the trunks, and caving in huge pieces of sheet metal. When the brutish Winterpole agents were finished, hardly anything remained of the incredible chomping devices. Bits of broken shrapnel bobbed on the ocean surface, blending in with the rest of the trash.

Rick felt his chest burning up. He hadn't been this angry since Evie had deleted his saved game of *Animon Hunters* after he'd finally reached the last boss. But this was so much worse. His dad's dream, destroyed in an instant.

George Lane cradled the Buhana of Paradise, disturbed by the sight. "All my dreams . . . my years of work . . . gone. . . ."

Rick clenched his fists, refusing to cry. He wasn't sure whom he was more incensed at, Winterpole or his father. Even if they had busted him on a technicality, Dad had broken the rules, and that was wrong. Still, Rick felt an obligation to fix this latest disaster, for the sake of his mom and his family's legacy. He was pretty good with technicalities too, and if there was a way to get his dad out of this mess, he would find it.

3

THE TRIP HOME HAD LEFT A SOUR TASTE IN EVIE'S MOUTH, AND NOT JUST BECAUSE SHE HAD EATEN an entire bag of Super Lemons to make herself feel better. After her dad's arrest and the awful destruction of his cool inventions, it was clear Winterpole had gone too far. Their absurd regulations had caused her dad countless problems, scuttled a bunch of projects, and slowed down scientific progress. As her mother would say, it was UN-AC-CEPTABLE.

Once the Winterpole agents commandeered the *Roost*, Mister Snow escorted Evie, Rick, and Dad back home to Switzerland. It was cold and cramped in the Winterpole hovership, and Evie couldn't help but think that 2-Tor was lonely piloting the *Roost*, which limped along behind them like a stray animal looking for a new home.

The hoverships came in low over the Rhone—just a few meters above the river. A pair of fishermen stopped to watch the giant tree fly by. Evie usually thought it was fun to wave at people staring at the airborne *Roost* in disbelief, but with all that had happened, she wasn't in the mood.

As they followed the river, Lane Mansion appeared atop a distant hill overlooking the city of Geneva.

Mister Snow sighed at the sight of it. "Lane, I cannot fathom this avian obsession of yours. Even your house looks like the outstretched wing of a bird."

George Lane ignored the observation, but Evie squinted, trying to see what Mister Snow meant. Light danced across the outside of the glass-and-steel mansion. She supposed it did look a little like a bird's wing.

The hovership touched down on the rooftop landing pad next to the aviary, a jungle gym of covered alcoves and bathing pools that housed the family's impressive collection of birds. At the sound of the hover engines, the birds went nuts, squawking in a feather fury. The aviary was one of Evie's favorite places in the house. She had always loved the birds her parents had rescued on their journeys around the world.

But now the sight only made Evie grimace like a gorilla without any bananas. It was a painful reminder of her dad's crime and Winterpole's merciless punishment.

Evie hopped out of the hovership in time to see 2-Tor swing the *Roost* upright and plant its roots down in the front yard.

Rick followed his sister out of the hovership, his concern for their dad apparent on his face. Evie slung her arm over his shoulder, and he returned her embrace. It seemed like Rick was the only person who understood what she was going through. Seeing Dad in trouble was the worst feeling in the world.

Her father stumbled down the exit ramp, bickering with Mister Snow. The Winterpole agent carried a bucket of murky blue liquid. He reached his hand inside and pulled out what looked like a sleek, dripping octopus, tentacles slick with lubricant and dangling like sausages.

"Ewww!" Evie grimaced.

"Gross!" Rick exclaimed.

Their dad agreed. "Mister Snow, is this really necessary?"

"Company Order 12-72 dictates that it is, in fact, *necessary*," Mister Snow replied, savoring every nasty word. "Winterpole has placed you under house arrest. This squid-cuff will monitor your location at all times. Under no circumstances are you to leave the premises of this house."

"What if we ignore your stupid rules?" Evie said.

"Failure to comply with Winterpole restrictions inevitably results in harsher penalties. In some cases, we send violators to Winterpole labor programs. We're always looking for eager—or not-so-eager—recruits to assist with filing at our home office. We have a back order of nine billion requests for everything from chewing gum factory purchases to armadillo skydiving instructor licenses to applications for permission to tie one's shoes. The shoe-tying requests alone fill the entire Reykjavík warehouse."

"Nine . . . billion?" Rick asked in disbelief.

Mister Snow had said he was just doing his job, but something about the smirk on his face told Evie that he relished this part of his work a little too much. "Our goal is to reach ten billion by Arbor Day! Now, of course, for a rule breaker as prolific as your father, a more serious punishment may be in order. If he violates the terms of his house arrest, Winterpole will take him to the Prison at the Pole."

Evie's insides felt as cold as the candy bars she sometimes put in the freezer. She'd only heard rumors about the Prison at the Pole, but she knew it was a place she never wanted to visit. Prisoners were supposedly kept in blocks of ice to ensure they wouldn't escape, with nothing to eat except frozen sardines. According to the stories, anyone who had ever attempted to find the prison had met with disappointment. It was said that the compound was carved out of an enormous iceberg that floated off the coast of Antarctica, and so it never stayed in one place, always eluding the attention of those who were desperate to find their imprisoned loved ones.

Worst of all, no one who had been sent to the Prison at the Pole had ever returned.

Her dad tried to reassure them. "Don't worry, kids. I'm not going to the pole. I'll just stay here for the time being."

At that, Mister Snow slapped the squid-cuff over Dad's leg. The tentacles wrapped around him like a snap bracelet, but with a loud, wet *SLURRRRRP!* The squishy texture of the tentacles hardened, and the color turned from silver to slate, forcing George's leg rigid. He grunted in pain.

Evie ran to his side. "Dad! Are you all right?!"

Under the squid-cuff's translucent skin, colored alert lights blinked their readings. Wires fed data from the tentacles' suction cups back to the microprocessor brain located in the big floppy part, which Evie thought she remembered was the technical term for a squid's head. If Evie's father made any attempt to leave Lane Mansion, the squid-cuff would constrict, cutting off all circulation to his leg.

"Who would invent such a horrible device?" Evie asked.

"Why, Lane Industries, of course," Mister Snow said proudly.

Dad winced and said, "We used to do some contract work for Winterpole, developing technology for their eco-protection unit. When I saw how inefficiently the place was run, we ended the contract. They've been hounding me ever since."

Mister Snow patted George on the head as if he were a small child. "Now, now, Mister Lane. It is you who insist on breaking the rules. We are merely the enforcers." And with that, Mister Snow reentered his hovership and blasted away.

Evie seethed. Winterpole had dealt a crushing blow to her family, and they didn't even care. There had to be something she could do to undo this injustice. Her family was good. They worked so hard to make the world a better place. Evie swore she would do everything in her power to right this wrong.

Rick adjusted his glasses and squinted at the squid-cuff. "Though cruel, the technology behind this incapacitator is fascinating."

Dad grunted in pain. "Thanks, Rick. I'll take that . . . *unff* . . . as a compliment."

Evie glared at Rick. "Why don't you think less about how

fascinating it is and more about how to get it off our dad?"

"Good idea, Evie. Let's head down to my workshop and find a solution together." Dad turned the wheel on the rooftop access hatch and opened it, revealing the spiral stairs that led down into Lane Mansion. The birds squawked loud goodbyes as he descended into the house, Evie and Rick following closely behind.

Lane Mansion was a long but oddly narrow building that stood ten stories tall. Spiral staircases and secret passageways led to the various floors, and Dad was always encouraging the kids to come up with new ways to get around the estate. For example, Evie's bedroom was directly above Rick's. They had installed a fireman's pole connecting the two, so Evie could quickly descend into Rick's room—usually to ask Rick about some homework problem or to borrow a video game.

Down the stairs the family went, passing by the master bedroom, the game room, Rick's and Evie's rooms, the living room, the dining room, and the front hall, and into the basement. When they reached the sub-basement, Evie's father pushed open a door, exiting the stairwell and entering his home workshop.

The walls were lined with broken computers, machine parts, and every imaginable tool from a micro-needle to a chainsaw. Wires were piled on the workbench like a giant collection of candy-colored worms. A few of the birds from the aviary had broken into the workshop and were perched on some of the equipment shelves. Bruce, their pink cockatoo, and Spruce, their cerulean warbler, were circling each other near the ceiling.

"Wark! Wark! Waaaaaaaark!" Bruce said, agitated. Evie reasoned that he probably didn't like how grumpy the humans were acting.

A scale model of one of the garbage chompers stood on two sawhorses in the middle of the workshop. Looking like he had eaten more bags of Super Lemons than Evie had in her whole life, Evie's dad grabbed an oil-stained sheet and threw it over the model. The weight of the sheet knocked one of the sawhorses aside, sending the mini garbage chomper crashing to the floor.

"Dad! Are you okay?" Evie raced forward to help him.

"I'm fine." He slumped down in a heap. "Evie, Rick, would you do me a favor? I'm not going to be able to get this squid thing off me, but down in the sub-sub-basement I have a bottle of high-tech skin spray. It should help me conceal this tentacled monstrosity from your mother once she returns from her business trip. Can you fetch it for me? I'm going to try to figure out how to shower with this thing."

"Sure, Dad," Evie replied, then she and Rick ran down a flight of stairs to the sub-sub-basement.

"I don't like how Dad is hiding what happened from Mom," Rick told her once they were out of earshot. "She deserves to know."

"You know how she is—you can't tell her. We'll all get in trouble. Even you."

Their argument abruptly ended as they reached the

sub-sub-basement, where their father conducted some of his more explosive experiments. Careful of their footing, Rick and Evie climbed over a barricade of shrapnel and mangled furniture to enter the room.

The chamber was dark, and the wooden floor groaned like a sick wombat when Evie stepped on it. In the center of the room was a large star of charred flooring, the shadow of some forgotten detonation. On the far side of the room, Evie spotted the bottle of skin spray on a shelf. She promptly forgot about the charred floor as she ran to get the spray for her father.

"Evie, wait!" Rick cried out. But it was too late.

As her foot touched the burnt flooring, the wood made a cracking sound like thin ice breaking, and then splinters flew and Evie tumbled into darkness.

DANGLING FROM AN ORANGE EXTENSION CABLE, RICK LOWERED HIMSELF THROUGH THE HOLE IN the floor of the sub-sub-basement. The first aid kit he'd just picked up was tucked under his arm. "Evie! Are you hurt? I brought antibacterial gel."

Evie had landed one level down on a pile of jumbled tarps. "Aw, Rick, you raced down here to rescue me. That's sweet."

For a moment, deep worry was etched on his face. Then it faded. "I know. I'm always saving your reckless neck when you get in trouble."

"Aaaand you ruined it. Great. Come on, hero. Let's check out this secret room."

They were in a part of the mansion they had never seen before. It looked like a storeroom for their dad's retired experiments. Storage crates and rusted shelves formed a grid that crisscrossed like city streets. Dusty picture frames and broken robots were strewn around like discarded marionettes. At the far end of the room was a metal desk pushed against a concrete wall with an old desktop computer and a few data discs covered in dust.

One of the discs caught Rick's eye. Written on the top in big, bold marker was *EDEN*. He picked up the disc to inspect it, but Evie snatched it from his hand and started cleaning off the dust with her shirt.

"Don't scratch it!" Rick wailed as he powered up the computer. Evie rolled her eyes and popped in the disc.

A video began playing. The bad computer graphics in the animation made it look like an old movie. Rick had rendered better-looking CGI on his laptop.

The video showed a desert under a hot sun, with smooth, shifting dunes. The images changed to colorful rain forests as a voiceover explained. "Terraforming. Literally, it means 'shaping the earth.' It's an advanced form of eco-modification through which scientists can alter the atmosphere and substance of an inhospitable environment to make it habitable for humans."

Evie massaged her temples. "All these big words are making my brain hurt."

"Shh . . ." Rick hushed his sister. "I think I get it. Using science, terraforming can transform a desert into a forest."

The video showed a map of the world where all the deserts were slowly turning green. The voiceover continued. "Large areas of the earth are uninhabitable, like the great Sahara Desert and the entire icy continent of Antarctica. We wanted to create a chemical compound that would kick-start the earth's natural growth processes, to bring dirt to flower, and garbage to life."

An image of Rick's father appeared on the screen, looking no older than twenty years of age. "Hi! I'm George Lane. Under the tutelage of my thesis advisor, Doctor Evan Grant, I have developed the Eden Compound, a remarkable new substance that will allow users to convert trash into organic matter."

The video switched to a computer-generated image of a garbage dump—miles of trash heaped in big mounds, with the expected empty boxes and discarded food.

Dad's voice continued. "In small doses, the Eden Compound is capable of transforming garbage into organic matter—plastic into dirt, cardboard into grass, rotten food into fresh water. Landfills could become public parks or even farmland."

An airplane flew over the landfill, spraying a mist of Eden Compound onto the garbage, transforming it into a verdant landscape.

The video abruptly cut out, and the computer returned to the desktop screen. Rick's mind flew faster than the *Roost* at top speed. The Eden Compound. He repeated the name out loud. "The Eden Compound. Think of the possibilities."

"Every trash dump transformed instantly into fresh, fertile land. Gardens from garbage." Evie was so excited she hopped up and down, accidentally knocking Rick's glasses off his face. He crawled around on the floor looking for them.

Dad's garbage chompers may have been destroyed, but with the Eden Compound, they could transform the Great

Pacific Garbage Patch into an island the size of Texas (or at least the size of Rhode Island). Just like Dad dreamed.

Evie tapped a finger against her lips contemplatively. "If we made that island using Dad's formula, we would own it—a place where Vesuvia Piffle couldn't ruin my life at school, where Dad could set up a lab and conduct experiments in peace. We could provide a sanctuary to the birds and other animals of the world that have lost their homes. Just think of all the amazing things we could do."

Rick imagined building his own castles and villages like in his city-simulator video game. He thought about getting every bird on the island to follow his commands. He could help his dad with wild experiments and even conduct some of his own.

"Of course," Evie reasoned, "if we made Trash Island, Winterpole would still be sticking their noses into our business."

With that realization, Rick's mind peeled back another layer of possibilities. "Wait a minute, Evie. Winterpole bylaws clearly state that they have jurisdiction over everything on all *seven* continents. But if we transform Trash Island, it would be big enough to be called a new continent. The eighth continent."

"You mean Winterpole wouldn't be able to tell us what to do? Ooooh, Rick! This is cool. This is cool-plus. We have to do this."

Rick, though quiet, felt his heart pound with the realization: Winterpole was the custodian of the technicality, and he was going to beat them *on a technicality*.

"But there's one thing I don't understand," Evie continued.

"One thing?" Rick asked with a wink.

"Okay, there a lot of things I don't understand, but there's one thing I don't understand about this. Where is the compound? I don't see it on the disc with the video. And where is this Doctor Grant who worked on the project with Dad? Have you ever heard of him? I haven't."

Rick was too embarrassed to admit that he never had, either. "You're right. Where are these forested landfills? Why was Dad not already using the compound to terra-form the garbage patch? Obviously, they never finished the project, and there has to be a reason why. We should consult all the top search engines, public library data-bases, and maybe look into hiring a private investigator. That should help us answer these questions."

"Or we could just ask Dad." Evie pointed at the ceiling. "He's right upstairs."

"Good point." Rick stuck the disc in his breast pocket and followed Evie back to their father's workshop. Breathlessly they explained what they'd discovered in the sub-sub-sub-basement while waving the disc in his face.

Dad leaned back in his chair, taking in what his children had just said. He rubbed his leg sorely. There were signs of a dark rash forming under the squid-cuff.

"So what do you think, Dad?" Evie was so excited she hopped from foot to foot, looking like 2-Tor did when he was leaking hydraulic fluid.

"What do I think?" George echoed. "I think that using the Eden Compound to create an eighth continent is a wonderful idea, children."

Her dad's encouragement made Evie feel like her spirits were about to take off.

"But unfortunately, I only have half the formula."

And then those spirits promptly drove off the end of the runway.

"Half the formula?" Rick parroted.

"Oh yes, it's been years since I've seen the other half. I used to dream about the Eden Compound all the time, but that was before I boarded up the sub-sub-sub-basement. Not that I'm saying you should worry about the hole in the floor."

Evie began to turn red. "Hole? I prefer to think of it as . . . impromptu renovations."

"Ha! I hadn't thought about that. And besides, patching the floor up will give me something to do while I'm stuck in this house."

"Dad, Evie, can we focus, please?" Rick said, interrupting their exchange. "Why didn't you ever use the Eden Compound before now?"

George cast his eyes downward in regret. "One of our financial backers on the project was Mastercorp."

"The military contractor?" Rick asked.

George nodded. "When Mastercorp found out what we had discovered, they wanted to take the invention for themselves. They saw the Eden Compound as a weapon. If the compound could transform plastic and metal inside a garbage dump, why not the same materials on a battleship or an airplane? We wanted nothing to do with weapons of war, so we scrapped the project and broke up the formula so that I took half the notes and Doctor Grant took the other half. Without possession of both halves of the formula, no one can create the Eden Compound—not even us."

"Easy-peasy! All we have to do is go to Doctor Grant and get his half of the formula. Then we can create our own island, a new world of freedom and security!" Evie stood tall, thumping her chest like the politicians she had seen on TV. "The eighth continent! That's right, Rick, I'm stealing your name. So, where is Doctor Grant?"

"I have no idea," their father said.

"Oh." Evie's arms dropped to her sides.

"Alas, I haven't seen him since the day we abandoned the project, well before either of you were born. But Winterpole might know. When they got wind that we were working on an experiment that could change the face of the world, they kept a close eye on both me and Doctor Grant. Perhaps they have some record of his whereabouts in their headquarters."

A muscle in Rick's eye started to twitch. "We can't just walk into Winterpole Headquarters without a reason. They'll never let us in."

"We can sneak in! I'm already concocting a brilliant cover story for our entry." Evie's voice took on the tone of a narrator in a movie trailer. "When a man . . . is wrongly imprisoned . . . one daughter . . . and her nerdy brother . . . will do *whatever* it takes. This summer . . . a family in tatters . . .

a horrible injustice—"

Rick felt unsure about this plan, to say the least. "I dunno, Evie. No offense, but most of your ideas are pretty—"

"Terrible! Just terrible!" From the corner, 2-Tor, who had been quiet for some time, squawked. "Incoming communication from Melinda Lane. Please stand by for transmission."

In a panic, Dad threw a tarp over his lap, hiding the squid-cuff. Rick bit his tongue so he wouldn't shout. It still felt wrong for his father to be keeping his latest misdeed a secret.

The video screen in 2-Tor's stomach brightened, and the comforting face of Rick's mother appeared. The soft wrinkles around her warm brown eyes were hidden mostly by her glasses. Her dark hair was pulled back in a no-nonsense bun. She smiled as her video feed came online, but the grin quickly vanished.

"George! What are the kids doing home from school so early?"

"They're not home early, honey. They didn't go in at all today."

Dread filled up inside Rick like ink in a bottle. He remembered that he had missed a Latin quiz today while they were off saving the Buhana of Paradise. *Eheu.*

"Sorry, honey!" Dad continued. "We had important business to take care of in the North Pacific. The kids were a big help."

"But, George! They're supposed to be in class."

"2-Tor did an excellent job teaching them today. They didn't miss anything at school. And they were here helping their very accomplished father." Dad grinned. "Think of all the stuff they're learning from me!"

Mom groaned. "How are they going to develop healthy social lives if you're always pulling them out of their environment?"

Dad stammered, "I, well, um . . ."

Waving at the camera, but all business, Mom said, "Hi, kids. Listen. You have to go to school tomorrow. No exceptions. I'm going to check in with the headmaster, and if you're not both there in time for first period, all *three* of you are going to be in big, big trouble. Got it, George? Got it, kids? This is UN-AC-CEPTABLE."

Rick had argued with Dad for three hours the night before about the trip to the Buhana Jungle. He hadn't wanted to go. Now Mom was mad at him just as she always was at Evie.

"Tomorrow. First period. Or else. Okay, byeeeeeee!" She switched off the feed, and 2-Tor's belly went dark.

"You heard your mother," Dad said. "You gotta go to school tomorrow. That takes first priority."

"I heard her say we have to go to *first period*," Evie said with the sly smile that usually presaged Rick finding himself in unpleasant situations. "After that, all bets are off. We'll find a way to sneak out of school, and then a way to sneak *into* Winterpole Headquarters."

2-Tor wailed like a talking doll with a broken pull-string. "I must strongly protest against this—"

"And then," she said, turning to the robot, "we'll come

home and you can quiz us all you want. Okay?"

Their father's eyes sparkled with pride at Evie's discovery of the loophole. He lowered his voice. "Richard, Evelyn, listen to me. You are about to infiltrate the headquarters of an international police organization under false pretenses. You are going to search for a scientist who has been missing for over a decade. You are doing this in order to create a substance that could save the world or, in the wrong hands, destroy it. Your mission is next to impossible, and almost certainly dangerous. So while you are on your quest, I beg you, whatever you do, don't tell your mother."

5

THE BUS DRIVER'S VOICE BLATTED OVER THE INTERCOM: "STUDENTS. PLEASE EQUIP YOUR

backpacks and line up at the front of the bus. We are coming up on ISES."

Evie shouldered her backpack and pushed her way to the front of the line. School was a complete drag, but the trip there was the best part of her day.

Two boys in front of her were debating the merits of a new documentary film on the fall of the Roman Empire. "Come on, boys! We don't have all century!"

Rick hissed from behind her, "Evie! Leave them alone."

Evie didn't have time to be polite. As soon as they got to school, she would be in Vesuvia's territory. Evie shuddered just thinking about the awful things Vesuvia had done to classmates who had supposedly wronged her. One time a boy called Vesuvia's haircut "unusual." At first it looked like she was cool with it, but that afternoon a pack of pink robo-wolves *mysteriously* appeared and chased him around the playground. The boy ended up transferring to military school; he said he needed a less stressful environment. Then last year there was the girl who accidentally wore the same dress as Vesuvia on the first day of school. Vesuvia lit the offensive garment on fire. That girl's eyebrows never grew back right.

Evie shook like an industrial paint mixer. The eighth continent could not come soon enough. Then Evie could escape the International School for Exceptional Students and never go near Vesuvia Piffle again.

These final moments on the way to school might have been the last happy seconds she would ever have as a student at ISES, and she was not about to let a couple of yapping snails ruin it for her.

"Okay!" the driver said. "We're over the target. Go! Go! Go!"

The door folded open and kids started filing out, tumbling through hundreds of feet of open sky toward the school below.

Evie could hear Rick behind her, his teeth chattering like castanets. The first time Evie had parachuted out of the bus—really a jumbo octo-blade helicopter—her bones had turned to marmalade. Now, though, it was a thrill, as it was for every single one of her classmates. Everyone, that is, but Rick. When he jumped, he still screamed like a baby goat.

"Just remember that even though you're a big wimp, I still love you," Evie said to her brother.

Then she took a nosedive out the door.

The wind rushed past her ears as she plummeted toward

the ground below. From a thousand feet up, she could see her entire school. A hexagonal wall surrounded the mountaintop campus, which was dotted with weathered brick buildings. Bright morning sunlight reflected off the solar panels that shingled each roof. On the big lawn in the center of campus, students from an earlier chopper-bus chatted in small groups.

Evie straightened her body and aimed for the lawn. When she reached the correct height, Evie tugged the pull-string on her backpack, and an apple-red parachute billowed out. The sudden jolt snapped her forward, and a moment later she landed gracefully in a crowd of eighth-grade boys.

"Hiya!" Evie smiled at them. They snickered and walked away. Okay, that wasn't too abnormal. The boys at school usually thought Evie was kind of weird.

Seconds later, Rick landed beside her. His feet slipped, and he toppled into the mud.

"I'd give that landing a nine-point-two," Evie said sarcastically.

Rick wiped the mud off his glasses. "Don't worry. I have six changes of clothes just in case of emergencies like this."

"Oh, phew, that's a big relief."

"Yeah, I know, right? I really thought ahead."

"Yeah, I thought you might only have had *four*. Then you'd really have been in trouble."

"Four? Are you crazy? The school week has *five* days, and what if—" Rick paused as Evie started to snicker. "Very funny, Evie," he concluded. Then he shambled off.

"See you after first period," she replied with a mischievous smile.

Behind her, a girl shrieked. "No, Diana, you stupid toad! I want the cocoa butter scallops as an appetizer today at lunch. For my entree, I will have the spider maki—no, wait—the chateaubriand."

"Yes, Vesuvia. Of course, Vesuvia," Diana Maple said, tapping notes frantically into her phone.

Evie glanced over her shoulder, wondering if she'd been seen. There sat Vesuvia Piffle on a park bench with a gaggle of friends. She was the biggest egomaniac in the school, and that was saying something, considering this was the International School for Exceptional Students. ISES was an expensive high-tech academy for the children of the world's richest and most important people. Skydiving and chateaubriand were just a couple of the many perks.

Yes, the International School for Exceptional Students might have been a perfect place, if it weren't for the kids who studied there. Example A: Vesuvia Piffle. Her hair was so blond it was nearly white, and at age eleven the rumor was she had already had a nose job and two face-lifts. She looked like a movie star, plastic and perfect. She carried a purse instead of a backpack, inside of which was a little pink robot that was always beeping and sticking its head out. Today the little robot was a pink turtle. Last week it had been a pink ferret.

Diana, by contrast, was wearing a misbuttoned blouse

and a skirt that was on backward. She looked up from her phone as Evie tried to slink away. "Oh, hi, Evie. Good morning."

"Um, hi . . ." Evie glanced at Vesuvia to gauge her reaction. Her face was as impassive as a porcelain doll's.

The moment of silence that followed made Evie feel like she was an animal in a zoo that the other students had come to gawk at. Two of the girls in Vesuvia's gang whispered impassionedly to their esteemed leader, one in each ear. Vesuvia nodded slowly.

Evie tried to be diplomatic. "So, Vesuvia . . . about yesterday."

"Whatever do you mean, Evie? It's fine." Vesuvia smiled her movie star smile. "I know what it's like to have a daddy who is a complete loser. It's not your fault."

"Okay, ummm . . . uh, thanks. That's great. Err . . . see you later." Evie gave a little wave and ran away before Vesuvia could say anything else. That wasn't nearly as bad as Evie had feared. Vesuvia seemed almost cool about the whole thing.

She raced into the student center to swap out her parachute for some textbooks before first period. The halls were packed with students on their way to class, cramming for tests, dueling holo-dragons, finishing last night's homework, and gossiping. Never a dull moment at ISES.

When she reached her locker, Evie pushed her thumb against the scanner, and the locker popped open.

And that's when the avalanche happened. Filthy, stinking garbage poured out. Brown oranges and fuzzy mushrooms tumbled to the floor. A rotten tomato landed on her shoes.

A dozen students burst out laughing at the sight, pointing fingers and screeching like harpies. Evie shriveled.

An envelope hung from the top of her locker on a strip of tape. Inside was a note:

> *In honor of the wonderful memories we shared in the Buhana Jungle, I thought I would give you this souvenir as a token of my appreciation.*
>
> —V

Not knowing what to do, Evie fled, tears and legs both running as fast as they could to escape.

She sat in a stall in the girls' room and cried until the well went dry. After that humiliation, she could never show her face at this school again. Now she really had to complete her mission and make the eighth continent. She could never come back here.

Evie emerged to find the bathroom attendant standing there as stiffly as ever, like a "proper" servant, ignoring the puffy and soggy face of the girl who had been hiding on the toilet for twenty minutes.

"A moist towelette, Miss Lane? Some mouthwash? Perhaps a spritz of perfume?"

"No thanks, Danushka," Evie said sadly, washing her hands in the automatic sink. Even the Bach preludes that played when she held her fingers under the faucet did little to improve her mood.

As she closed the door to the restroom, it occurred to Evie that she was twenty minutes late for first period. Not only was her social life devastated but a trash stasher had a bazooka to grind with her, and she might have jeopardized the mission to build the one thing that could get her out of ISES purgatory.

She poked herself in the forehead. "You had one job, Evie. One job!" She raced to her first-period class and slipped into her seat.

The instant she made contact with her chair, her teacher launched into a big lecture about punctuality and professionalism and how Evie Lane had just displayed neither. On a normal day this would have been the most humiliating thing ever—literally her entire class could hear Evie being reprimanded—but today it was nothing compared to the crazy that was radiating from Vesuvia two desks over.

After the scolding, Vesuvia leaned over to Diana and whispered something in her ear. Diana turned to Evie and said, "Vesuvia wants to know if you found her gift and if you appreciated it."

Evie leaned in, refusing to be intimidated. "You can tell Vesuvia that I appreciate that she is a sociopath."

"Of course I am!" Vesuvia cheeped with a flip of her hair. "I'm the most social person in the whole school. But it's too late for compliments, Peevy Evie. I'm still going to ruin your life."

The second half of first period was the longest twenty-five minutes of Evie's existence, and the moment the bell rang, she jumped up and raced out of the room, not giving Vesuvia an extra second to insult her. She nabbed Rick in the hall on the way to second period.

"You're so lucky that Mom checked our class attendance at the end of first period instead of the beginning," Rick said as they wove their way through the crowded school. "Where were you?"

"I don't want to talk about it." Evie hung her head. "So things with Mom went okay? She confirmed that we were here?"

"Yeah," Rick conceded. "But that doesn't mean you should take risks like that."

Evie ignored his advice. "Follow me," she said, leading Rick out of the building and onto the finely manicured lawn where children played Segway polo after lunch. The other kids totally ignored Evie—probably at Vesuvia's command—as she and her brother crossed the field.

"Evie, maybe this is a bad idea," Rick said. "I have a three-page worksheet due in second period."

"Sorry, Ricky. Second period is canceled." With a roar of white-hot hover engines, the *Roost* shot over the school like a fiery comet, assuming that burning space ice took on the shape of giant trees. "We're taking a field trip to Winterpole."

6

THE WINTERPOLE HEADQUARTERS WAS A MASSIVE BUILDING ON THE OPPOSITE SIDE OF GENEVA FROM Lane Mansion. At a distance, the concrete megastructure resembled an immense ant mound—a big dome pocked with alcoves and dark windows. Its halls and chambers went deep underground in a winding network.

2-Tor brought the *Roost* in for a smooth landing in front of the building. Rick and Evie exited the vehicle, each carrying a stack of papers. These documents were the permission slips necessary to enter Winterpole's main facility.

Rick was so worried he wouldn't have been surprised if his nose started spontaneously bleeding. Winterpole Headquarters. So much could go wrong. What if he'd made mistakes filling out the permission slips he'd downloaded from the Winterpole website? What if some administrator woke up on the wrong side of the bureaucracy and denied them admission irrespective of the forms? Worst of all, what if his brash sister's penchant for recklessness bungled the whole operation?

"Trust me," she'd assured him on the ride over. "No one wants to build the eighth continent more than me. I'll be careful."

Well, there's a first time for everything, Rick thought optimistically as he and Evie approached the entrance to the building. The wide glass doors slid open with a hiss. Refrigerated air billowed into the warm morning like it was fleeing a crime.

The vast marble hall beyond the entrance looked like the inside of an igloo, its smooth walls leading up to a domed ceiling of marble panels that resembled packed snow. More doors than Rick could count led out of the room. At the center of the space was a bucket-shaped desk. A single administrator, in a crisp blue uniform, sat inside the bucket, towering over the immense empty space. A set of steep stairs led down from the desk. Save this one man, with matted black hair and Oreo-shaped sunglasses, the entire room was deserted.

Dozens of old-fashioned candlestick telephones hung from the ceiling. The administrator had one of the cones clutched to his ear. He nodded and muttered into the receiver, ignoring the Lane children completely.

Rick and Evie crossed the threshold, shivering in the wintry air.

BWWWWAAAAAAAAAAAAAAAAAAAAAAMMMM!!!!!!!

The Lane siblings froze in their tracks.

Rising from his chair, the administrator opened the door beside his desk and descended the stairs. With each step on the waxed floor, his smart leather shoes squeaked like a dying rat. He waddled across the room, taking his sweet time, until he stood before Rick and Evie.

"Two penalties!" the administrator said. Up close, Rick could see that he was incredibly short. "One for each of you. Don't you know there is a penalty for entering Winterpole Headquarters without permission?"

"We just got here," Rick said.

"And already two penalties! You must be wicked children indeed." The administrator shoved his hand into his breast pocket and rooted around like he was looking for the toy at the bottom of a cereal box.

Rick and Evie exchanged a knowing glance. This guy was not going to make getting into Winterpole easy.

The administrator withdrew a stack of stapled tickets and scribbled on two of them furiously. He tore them off. *Rip! Rip!* He handed one to Rick and one to Evie. "There you go. In the future I hope you will be more respectful of authority and protocol."

Rick felt like he had forgotten to charge his Game Zinger before a long trip. Two minutes after trusting Evie and already he had a penalty from Winterpole. What would his mother say? Would the teachers at ISES put this on his permanent record? It would certainly have an effect on his ability to get into a top university.

Evie nudged him. "Rick, snap out of it. You're not going to jail. It's just a piece of paper."

That was easy for her to say. She had lined a whole set

of drawers with all the demerits she'd received at school. One more didn't mean anything to her.

The administrator squeaked on his heels and retreated to his desk. Up the stairs he went, then he plopped back down into his seat.

With that interruption behind him, and trying to shake the feeling that his future was in jeopardy, Rick started toward one of the doors.

BWWWWAAAAAAAAAAAAAAAAAAAAAAMMMM!!!!!!!

The alarm blared. The administrator stood up from his chair, opened the door in his desk, and started the whole cycle again.

"Two penalties! Don't you listen when people talk to you?"

"What did we do this time?" asked Rick. He started to gasp like a fish on land.

The administrator handed out more tickets. "You still have not asked permission to enter Winterpole Headquarters. Without permission, every step you take in this building is considered trespassing and a violation. Do you want me to throw you out of here?"

Rick hefted his stack of papers and said, "That will not be necessary. We have our permission slips right here."

BWWWWAAAAAAAAAAAAAAAAAAAAAAMMMM!!!!!!!

Startled, Evie dropped her permission slips with an echoing *whump!* A few loose sheets whirled through the air like feathers on the wind.

BWWWWAAAAAAAAAAAAAAAAAAAAAAMMMM!!!!!!!

Evie ran around the lobby, gathering up the papers.

MATT LONDON

"Three penalties! You really are naughty, *naughty* little children."

"Now, wait a second," Rick said. "We are asking permission to enter the headquarters. That is what you just told us to do!"

"One penalty is for this girl making an unseemly mess of Winterpole property. The other two are for failing to request permission to submit a permission slip to a Winterpole administrator."

Rick's head was starting to hurt. "Wait a minute. You mean we need permission to ask for permission?"

"Of course you need permission to ask permission, you, you, you, you . . . children!" the administrator stammered. "The rule is clearly stated in Winterpole Statute 47-X3. Don't you know ANYTHING?"

Evie snapped. "That's a stupid rule!"

BWWWWAAAAAAAAAAAAAAAAAAAAMMMM!!!!!!!

"Evie!" Rick wiped his face to hide his embarrassment. "You're not helping."

The administrator returned to his desk and sat down in a huff.

Rick cleared his throat. The noise echoed off the walls of the cavernous lobby. "Um . . . excuse me. Mister Administrator?"

"What is it?" the administrator asked.

"We have these permission slips to enter Winterpole Headquarters. May we have permission to submit them to you for review?"

The administrator ambushed them with a courteous smile. "Winterpole reviews all permission slips submitted. It is but one of the many services we extend to the people of Earth. Please come up to the desk and submit your permission slips."

Evie picked up her reassembled stack of papers and blew a loose lock of hair out of her face. "Suck-up," she muttered, glaring at her brother.

Rick shrugged and approached the desk, each footstep creaking on the floor like he was walking on a pond that was barely frozen over. He had to stand on his toes to place his stack of papers in front of the administrator, then he did the same with Evie's, because she was too short to reach.

The administrator flipped through the papers. "What is your business at Winterpole?"

Rick was proud of the compromise he had come to with Evie regarding their cover story. "We are here to review the statutes to see if there is anything we can do to help our father, George Lane. He is under house arrest."

"Oh, yes. I heard about that. Poachers are a deplorable bunch. No wonder you children are so poorly behaved."

"He's not a poacher!" Evie said. "He was saving that bird. My dad has never killed an animal in his life."

The administrator ignored the outburst. "Well, I don't know what you expect to find in the statutes to undo the punishment for your father's reprehensible crime, but these requests seem to be in order. It will take several weeks before we can complete our evaluation. Each error will result in a penalty. We reserve the right to revoke admittance if any errors are found. In the meantime, you are granted permission to enter Winterpole Headquarters."

"Thank Tesla!" Rick breathed a huge sigh of relief. His mission objectives were complete. Time to advance to the next level.

"Where can we find access to Winterpole's computer database?" Evie asked the administrator.

He didn't look up from his paperwork. "Any of the doors on the western curve of the lobby will lead you there . . . eventually."

Rick and Evie hurried across the room, Rick grabbing his sister's arm before she could sprint forward. Rick was certain running would result in another penalty. He shook his head, hoping his sister got the message to keep both feet on the ground, then chose a door that looked promising.

BWWWWAAAAAAAAAAAAAAAAAAAAMMMM!!!!!!!

Now what?

The administrator blushed. "Sorry! That was my mistake. Hand slipped and hit the buzzer. One penalty for me."

Rick and Evie left the lobby as fast as they could.

The hall was no warmer than the foyer had been. On the plus side, Rick and Evie were alone. The minus side was that the walls, doors, and floor were painted the same dull beige of a forgotten decade. It was impossible to tell one place from another.

"Which way is the data room?" Evie asked.

Rick had no idea where it was, but he didn't want his

sister knowing that. "I think it's this way. Follow me."

The hall bent in a long curve. Doors branched off the corridor, but most had old-fashioned padlocks. Whenever they located an unlocked door, Evie opened it eagerly. But each time all they found inside was paperwork stacked to the ceiling.

"You would think they would recycle some of this stuff," Rick said. "Or at least make digital copies. They must spend a fortune on ink."

At the end of the hall, the kids saw a man and a woman in business suits come around the corner. Rick recognized the man instantly. "It's Mister Snow!" he whispered. "Quick, hide!"

The kids darted into the nearest room.

Glancing around, Rick couldn't believe their good luck. "We're inside Winterpole's database access room!" he exclaimed. Several white cubes—which Rick recognized as archaic computer monitors—hung from the ceiling, swaying gently, each with keyboards dangling. Rick tapped the spacebar on one of the keyboards a few times, and the screen brightened.

"Awesome sauce!" Evie pumped her fist victoriously. "And now we search for Doctor Grant."

One thing that Rick and Evie could agree on was that computers were the spellbooks of the real world. By coding a computer program, Rick could make the machine do anything he dreamed of, just like magic. When he was writing a piece of code, called a script, he felt like a genius wizard hunched over a cauldron at the top of a tall tower.

His latest incantation, which was really just a quickly scripted program that chugged through the data in the Winterpole network, was one of his usual masterpieces, but the search moved at a crawl on the obsolete computer. Then the results started to come in. Most of the files were old reports from the days when Winterpole monitored Doctor Grant. At around five years ago, the updates began to get much less frequent. "I guess he got harder to track," Rick mused as he examined the files. The later reports were little more than rumored sightings of Doctor Grant in random places around the world.

"Hey, Rick, check this out!" Evie had located a different computer and was exploring the system. While Rick's programming style was meticulous, Evie never studied or practiced, so her coding was rough, aggressive, and prone to errors, much like Evie herself. "I found the master list of every infringement of Winterpole regulations. Look, here's Dad's file."

"Evie, don't touch anything." Rick did not have time for her dangerous curiosity.

She scrolled through her father's infractions. "Wow. This is longer than one of 2-Tor's lectures."

Rick was about to ask Evie what she was talking about when he discovered the most recent report on Doctor Grant tucked away in an unmarked subfolder. "Here we go. Doctor Evan Grant was working on a top-secret construction project two years ago. It looks like he was in—"

"You won't believe this! Dad's profile is available for editing. All I have to do is delete his infractions, and he should have a clean slate. Isn't that awesome?"

"Evie, I said do not—"

But it was too late. With one push of the delete key, George Lane's many infractions vanished from the database. Evie grinned at her skeptical brother. Rick watched in horror as her computer screen turned the color of fresh blood, and all the lights in the database access room went dark.

Hazard lights along the floor flashed. Sirens blared so loud Rick felt like his head was going to pop like an alien puss bug.

"EMERGENCY! EMERGENCY! UNAUTHORIZED DATABASE ALTERATION DETECTED. DISPATCH SECURITY TO D.A.R. L1."

Rick shot Evie an accusing glare.

Evie shrugged. "Maybe they're talking about someone else?"

IN EVIE'S DEFENSE, SHE REALLY HAD WANTED WHAT WAS BEST FOR THEIR DAD. THE OPPORTUNITY to undo all his past infractions had been staring her in the face. She figured any kid in her position would have done the same. After all that business with the annoying administrator, they hadn't had any trouble walking right in. Security seemed lax. How could she have known the slightest change to Winterpole records would result in a full-blown military lockdown?

"Are you out of your mind?!" Rick screamed, frantically trying to finish collecting the data he had found on Doctor Grant. "Winterpole has rules against using a DVORAK keyboard! You didn't think there would be rules against altering their official disciplinary records?"

"Well, excuse me, Mister Perfect! I didn't realize that the Child of the Year would be so quick to let his father wither away under house arrest when the answer to all his family's problems is staring him in the face!"

Rick grabbed her by the hand and ran for the door. He

fumbled for the doorknob in the dim light.

"Ow! Hey, lemme go!" Evie said.

"Gladly," Rick said. "Does that mean I can leave you here?"

Evie was quiet. Memorizing the dictionary sounded like more fun than staying to say howdy to Winterpole security.

They burst into the hall, looking for the closest exit. Down the corridor, two guards in white jumpsuits with matching domed helmets raised what looked like blue fire extinguishers. "Hey, you kids! Freeze!"

The lead guard squeezed the handle of his weapon. Bright blue water flew toward Rick's head.

Evie grabbed her brother and tugged him out of the way. And just in time. The water hit the door and froze solid on contact, locking it with cobalt ice.

The other guard gave his companion a skeptical glance. "Really, Larry? 'Freeze'? You spend all weekend coming up with that clever pun?"

Larry frowned, embarrassed. "Gosh, Barry. I don't know. It seemed appropriate in the moment."

Barry shook his head in dismay. "Winterpole is never going to shake its reputation as a cold, icy, monolithic organization if we can't get past the obvious connotations associated with its name. Now, let's think of something that isn't obvious and that better represents the ideals of our esteemed employer."

"Hurry!" Larry shouted.

Barry nodded in approval. "Not bad. 'Hurry.' It says we are quick to respond to any violations of Winterpole statutes, and it contradicts the inaccurate assumption that we move at glacial speed."

"No, I mean *hurry*! Those kids are getting away."

Down the hall, Evie and Rick had used the guards' conversation to bolt around the corner.

"Oh . . . " Barry said.

Evie and Rick raced through the complex, breathing hard. The floors were waxed so smoothly that their shoes skidded a bit with each step. "I thought you said no sudden movements?" Evie taunted in between slipping and sliding.

"Yeah, I changed my mind. RUN!"

Evie didn't need to be told twice. She quickly picked up her pace, pumping her legs as fast as they would go. Rick matched his sister stride for stride. In between labored breaths he called out, "To answer your earlier question, Evie, I do want to help Dad. That's why I entered Winterpole Headquarters under false pretenses to hack into their computer database. And that's why I want to terraform the Great Pacific Garbage Patch and make the eighth continent, just like you."

"Well, when you put it *that* way!" Evie veered around a corner and pushed down another identical hallway. The corridors all looked the same. Evie would have had an easier time finding her way in one of the world's many trash-tangled rain forests. Rick didn't seem so sure of himself, either, but her stay-at-home brother was leading the way for once, so she trusted his instincts.

They rounded another corner. Mister Snow was leaning

against the wall and enjoying a moment's peace. He looked like he was savoring every bite of the iceberg lettuce wrap he was eating for lunch. (Presumably, Winterpole had penalties for eating any other kind of lettuce.) Mister Snow dropped his food when he saw the Lanes.

A door opened, and the lobby administrator skidded into the hall. "There they are! The intruders! Two hundred penalties! Stop where you are!"

The administrator ran toward Rick and Evie just as Mister Snow bent to pick up his lunch. The two grown-ups collided, stumbling on the slick, waxy floor. Their legs went out from under them, and for a brief second they looked like two graceful swimmers embracing underwater.

Then the illusion was broken, and they tumbled to the floor in a heap.

"Get them!" the administrator groaned.

Mister Snow and the administrator were piled in front of the door to the lobby, blocking the exit. Thinking fast, Evie searched for a clue on one of the doors that would allow them to escape from Winterpole Headquarters.

When nothing obvious presented itself, Evie settled for the next best thing.

"Wild guess!" she cried out loud, and pulled Rick through the nearest door.

They were in a dark closet that was so tiny they had to smoosh together to fit.

"Where's the light?" Rick asked.

"Feel around for it," Evie instructed.

The kids ran their hands over the walls, searching for any protrusions that might have been light switches. After a few seconds, Evie's fingers wrapped around a metal handle.

"Triple-seven jackpot!" Evie said, tugging on the handle.

The handle did not operate the lights, but it did operate the trapdoor below the children's feet. They plummeted into a dark chute that twisted down into the basement of Winterpole Headquarters.

Cold air rushed past Evie's ears. Her hair flew wild. She kicked out her feet to try to slow her descent, but the walls of the chute were slippery.

"WAAAAAAAH! I'm falling!" Rick wailed. The echo of his cries chased them down the chute.

Some distance into the tunnel, they saw a small square of amber light. It grew larger as they approached, and before they could react, they flew out of the chute and tumbled several feet through the air before falling onto a soft cushion of—

"Paperwork!" Evie cheered with relief as she threw crumpled stationery into the air. "I never thought I would be so happy to see paperwork!"

But Rick wasn't paying attention. He rose, awed, and walked to the edge of the narrow platform where they'd landed. Evie followed his gaze.

They were in an underground cavern so large she couldn't see the far end of it. In the air before them, inverted rails twisted together like a clump of leftover spaghetti. Countless foot-long claws hung from the rails and flew along the tracks, so fast Evie could barely see each individual one. The claws were clamped onto punchcards, which were then circulated through hundreds of exits out the sides of the cavern.

"What is it?" Evie asked in amazement.

"It's . . . it's a computer," Rick replied, the shock evident in his voice.

"A computer?" Evie repeated. "But computers are small. This . . . this is gi-mongous!"

"Back in the early days of information electronics, computers had to be gi-mongous, er . . . gigantic. *Gi-mongous* isn't a . . . Anyway, they used to be as big as a whole room. The only way to send data was to input it on a stack of punchcards like these. But computers never would have become what they are today if people had continued to use the punchcard system. Each card only carried a tiny bit of data. You would need fifteen thousand punchcards to represent the data in one megabyte."

"Uh, Rick, a megabyte is, like, not even one song."

"I know. Winterpole has been around since the 1950s, when punchcards were in use. I bet they had something in their bylaws that never let them upgrade to modern computer systems, so they're still using punchcards, but on an incredible scale. Billions and billions of punchcards."

"That's a lot."

"Billions and billions and billions and billions and billions and—"

"Okay, I get it." Evie rolled her eyes.

At the other end of the balcony, a door opened. Barry and Larry squeezed through and raised their icetinguishers.

"Hurry!" Larry said.

"Good idea." Evie grabbed her brother by the shoulder. "Let's go!"

"No, that's not what we meant!" Barry said. "You're supposed to stop. We have icetinguishers. 'Hurry' is just our battle cry."

"Rick, jump!" Evie nudged him toward the edge of the balcony.

"It's too high!" Rick wailed.

"Do it!"

Barry fired ice. Evie scooped up a handful of papers on the ground and threw them at the glob. The icy-blue goo hit the papers in midair, coating them. The papers fell to the floor and shattered.

"Now! Jump!" Evie said, taking Rick by the hand and vaulting off the balcony.

They grabbed onto one of the claws and were rushed along the rails, twisting through the air like flying squirrels.

"Don't let go," Evie said.

"Can't say that I'm planning to." Rick squeezed his eyes shut. "But, you know, if I fall, Mom is going to be so mad at you."

Evie snorted. "You don't have to tell me that."

The rails carried them past a row of windows that looked into Winterpole offices. Evie saw a man talking into a headset and playing golf on his desk. A lady in yoga pants was suspended upside down in a huge gyroscope, while an old bald man in a karate uniform vigorously chopped at her back with his hands.

In the last window, a girl stood talking to a woman. The woman wore a silver sash over her Winterpole uniform. Evie had never seen a sash like that before, but she assumed it was reserved for high-ranking members of the Winterpole executive board. But the Winterpole woman wasn't the one who had caught Evie's attention. It was the girl, who—in lieu of a sash—was wearing the fifth-grade uniform from the International School for Exceptional Students.

"Diana Maple?" Evie said in disbelief.

Diana Maple, best friend and henchwoman of the vile, vicious, and vindictive Vesuvia Piffle. Vesuvia was the number one reason, after saving her father, why Evie needed to start a new continent. She had to get away from wicked girls like her.

The woman and Diana turned to look at Evie and Rick as they flew past, hanging from their punchcard claw. "You?" Diana mouthed, her eyes wide.

Now Vesuvia would know they had been to Winterpole Headquarters.

Evie was sure nothing good would come of that.

8

THE OFFICE OF VESUVIA PIFFLE, SUPER-SECRET CEO OF THE MULTINATIONAL CONDO CORPORATION,

was on the forty-seventh floor of Condoco Tower, in the heart of Geneva's Rive Droite.

Everything in Vesuvia's office was plastic. Plastic chairs, plastic desk. The carpet was made of plastic fibers, and the pink robot cat rolling on the carpet was plastic. Even the windows, with their spectacular view of the city, were—you guessed it—plastic as a movie star's smile.

And why not? According to Vesuvia, plastic was the world's greatest material, derived from petrol, the world's greatest fuel. A diabolical sixth grader would be crazy not to drape herself in plastic and other unnatural materials. Vesuvia did. Her black dress pants were plastic. Her beloved pink jacket was squeaky plastic. Plastic clothes were great. She never got wet, and she loved how they caught the light.

She used a special hairspray of liquid plastic, which never failed to hold its shape and which made her blond curls shimmer. Sure, she got headaches sometimes, and the fumes made her quite dizzy, but that was a small price to pay for sublime hair.

"Hey, you, pipe down!" Vesuvia shrieked into the phone. Her father might be the public face of the company, but there was no doubt she was the one in charge. After all, the Condo Corporation board of directors hadn't made Vesuvia super-secret CEO for nothing. "Bradley, you listen to me, you bloated iguana. If I don't get a detailed report of what happened to the missing gallon of plasti-pulp on my desk by five p.m., I'm going to dunk you in plastic and use you as a coatrack!"

"But, Miss Piffle," her terrified assistant said over the phone. "The shipment was for over one million gallons of PP. Surely one missing gallon isn't worth a whole report."

"Did I ask for your life story?! Five p.m. The report, or a resignation letter. *Your choice.* Now, where are we on the New Miami Project?"

≈≈≈≈≈

Quiet as a stealth robot, Diana Maple crept into Vesuvia's office. Diana was the only person allowed to enter Piffle's Pink Power Center without permission. Vesuvia said that this was because Diana was her best friend. But by "friend," she meant "employee," and by "employee," she meant someone who did lots of work for Vesuvia but did not collect a salary or benefits.

It was worth it, though. Vesuvia had made Diana popular—something no other homely girl at ISES could claim. And it made her mother so proud to know that she was one of the cool kids. The happiness she felt knowing her mom didn't think Diana was an embarrassment was worth all the times Vesuvia made her ransom less socially endowed kids' bookbags for an extra dish of cafeteria panna cotta, or torment grown Condo Corp employees until they cried for their security blankets.

"Vesuvia! Hey, Vesuvia!" Diana whispered, wanting to get her "friend's" attention without disrupting her important business call.

Vesuvia didn't stop frothing at the mouth long enough to even look at Diana. "What do you mean, they rejected the proposal? New Miami is going to be the greatest city since Renaissance Venice. It'll be ten times better than the real Miami. A million times! There will be sea urchin kebabs for sale in the streets, and a floating arena where you can watch scuba gladiators battle sharks to the death! Juice bars where you can get a hundred-twenty-eight-ounce pink grapefruit spinach smoothie with a vitamin blast, and a double-decker ocean. Do you know what that means, Bradley? I'm going to build a platform over the ocean . . . and put an ocean on it! How freaking awesome is that? Double ocean all the way across the sky!"

Diana piped in again. "Vesuvia! There is something really important I have to tell you. It's about Rick and Evie Lane, and—"

"Local character?" Vesuvia snapped at the phone. "You keep saying those words, but what do they mean? You're telling me that the people of Nice, France, don't want me to bulldoze their boring town and put New Miami in its place? Why not? New Miami is so much cooler than that stinky town. They have a cheese shop. It's a shop where they sell *cheese*. You can buy that anywhere. Who would want to spread Gruyère on a cracker when they could be harpooning a shark while surfing on a double-decker ocean and drinking a smoothie?"

Vesuvia listened to Bradley's reply, then hurled her phone across the room. Diana ducked, and the phone struck the wall with a plastic thump. "Uh . . . Vesuvia . . ." Diana picked up the phone and scurried back to her. "I think I know how to solve your problem with New Miami."

Vesuvia snatched the phone and shouted into it. "That may have been a good excuse for my feckless father, the quote-unquote 'public' CEO of Condo Corp, but it won't work for me. That's why my grandmother ordered the board to appoint *me* as the real CEO, because she knows that I have the strength and the *guts* to keep all you necktie-wearing wimps from taking *no* for an answer."

Diana had lost her patience. All Vesuvia had to do was pay attention, and her problems would be solved. "Vesuvia! Listen to me. It's important!"

Despite her shouts, Vesuvia either didn't see her standing there or had decided to totally ignore her. "Humph," Diana sighed. She left the inner office and spoke to Vesuvia's secretary, Mrs. Lemone, a sweet old lady with colorful sweaters, whose desk was just outside the door. "Mrs. Lemone, I'm going to need the horn."

"Of course, dear," Mrs. Lemone said. "I know how she gets. Here you go."

Diana reentered the inner office wielding an enormous megaphone. She switched it on and spoke into it so loudly the entire plastic room thrummed. "VESUVIA! HANG UP THE PHONE. I NEED TO TALK TO YOU."

Normally the horn would get Vesuvia's attention, but today she was in an especially foul mood.

"VESUVIA! I BROUGHT THE SWISS ARMY DRUM BAND. THEY'RE RIGHT OUTSIDE. THEY WANT YOUR AUTOGRAPH."

"I said pink Skittles! My private jet will only have pink Skittles. They need to be the tropical kind, too. Blech. I hate this stupid mountain town I'm stuck going to school in. I miss the beach."

Diana sighed. This called for desperate measures. "VESUVIA! THERE'S A SPIDER ON YOUR SHOULDER!"

Vesuvia screamed so loudly it knocked the megaphone out of Diana's hands. Vesuvia dropped to the ground, clawing at her shoulder and shouting, "Get it off, get it off, get it off me! I hate spiders!"

Diana ran to her friend's side to calm her down. "Hey! Hey, it's okay. It's gone. The spider is gone. Calm down."

Vesuvia gulped lungfuls of frightened air. "I *hate* spiders."

"I know you do," Diana said. "Now, listen, I saw something when I was visiting my mom at work."

"Yuck! You went to Winterpole? Do you realize how many of my incredible condo construction projects they have vetoed with their stupid bylaws? Those bureaucrats are useless."

Diana's mom always said that Winterpole kept the world clean and organized, but it was not worth arguing with Vesuvia. It would just send her off on another tangent, after Diana had finally gotten her attention. "Earlier today, Rick and Evie Lane snuck into Winterpole Headquarters."

"You mean I haven't gotten those nerds to flee the country yet? Yuckfest."

"They tried to erase all the terrible crimes their father has committed from Winterpole records. And then I found this on the security cameras."

Diana pulled out her phone and played the video she'd downloaded from Winterpole's security camera archive. It showed a grainy image of Rick and Evie racing down a hallway in Winterpole Headquarters. The audio was scratchy, but they clearly heard Rick say, "And that's why I want to terraform the Great Pacific Garbage Patch and make the eighth continent, just like you."

"Terra-what the who now?" Vesuvia asked.

"That's what I said!" Diana replied. "So I did some research. Apparently, there's this giant island of trash in the middle of the Pacific Ocean."

"Yeah, so?" Vesuvia shrugged.

Diana continued, "I think Rick and Evie are trying to turn that garbage into a new landmass, a whole continent, like Australia, but without the kangaroos."

"Sounds like a waste of perfectly good plastic," Vesuvia said.

"Don't you get it? If they build a continent, they'll own it. No one will be able to tell them what to do."

Vesuvia growled, "Ooh, I want to decapitate teddy bears when people tell me what to do."

"Exactly! And with all that extra land, you could finally build New Miami—and you could do it without having to kick people out of their homes or needing to tear up existing environments or being forced to—" Diana stopped herself. She saw that Vesuvia's eyes had glazed over. "You could even build a *triple*-decker ocean."

Vesuvia bubbled with excitement. "I could create the most prettiest, perfect plastic place on the planet, and I would be that place's princess. Diana, alert the Piffle Pink Patrol and tell Daddy I won't be coming to dinner. I want that continent!"

9

THE WINTERPOLE SANITATION TRUCK PULLED INTO A MASSIVE GARBAGE DUMP OUTSIDE GENEVA.
It had a full load of office waste, broken computer punchcards, and cafeteria leftovers, so even the security guard at the front of the dump, who must have been accustomed to mysterious odors, held his nose and waved it inside.

Upon reaching the designated dump point, the truck backed up, tilted the container, and let the refuse fall.

The old diesel truck shifted gears, coughed smoke, and sputtered away.

A moment passed.

Evie burst out of the pile of steaming garbage, gasping for breath. "Bleeeeeyagh! My nose will never forgive me."

Beside her, Rick's head emerged like a gopher from a hole. He gagged, wiping brown ketchup from his eyes. "*I* will never forgive you. That was your worst idea since . . . well, not that long ago, actually." He removed the banana peel he had been wearing as a hat.

Evie ran her fingers through her hair, straining out

eggshells and yolk. As usual, Rick failed to appreciate her brilliance. They were lucky she had spotted the garbage chute while they were on Mister Punchcard's Wild Ride—it was the only way they could sneak out of Winterpole Headquarters without getting caught. "I got us out of there, didn't I?" she said.

Rick extracted himself from the pile, looking quite green. "We could have just walked out like normal people if you hadn't felt the urge to hack us into that mess."

"Aww, come on, Rick. Can't you admit that our high-speed chase was just a little fun?"

"No." Rick activated the homing beacon he had pro-grammed into his phone so that 2-Tor could find them. "I can't admit that."

Evie crossed her arms, showing off her confidence. "You're just jealous because I'm so cool-tastic."

"False. But Templeton thinks you're cool-tastic."

"Who's Templeton?" Evie asked, then turned her head to see a rat six inches away, staring her in the face.

"Squeak!" said the rat.

"Yipes!" Evie jumped out of the trash and ran to Rick. "Where'd he come from?"

The roar of hover engines drew their attention skyward. The *Roost* emerged from a cloud and circled the dump. Evie never tired of watching the *Roost* fly. It looked so impossible, with its broad trunk, long branches, and canopy of leaves blowing in the jet stream.

The tree lowered a long tube, which slurped Rick and

Evie up inside. They landed in the storage hold, where 2-Tor was waiting for them.

"By my bolts, children!" He flapped his metal wings. "My olfactory sensors must be going haywire."

"Nah," Evie said. "We just smell like garbage."

"It's Evie's fault, 2-Tor. For a bunch of reasons." He took a step away from his sister.

"My fault? If it weren't for me, you'd still be hanging from that punchcard like a crying monkey. 'Oh, boo-hoo-hoo. I don't think this was a good idea.'"

"It wasn't a good idea. None of this has been."

"I am most displeased with both of you," 2-Tor scolded. "Most displeased. You are behind on your studies. You each have five more hours of homework, and you are overdue for a pop quiz."

Evie stuck out her tongue. "A quiz? Is this really a good time?"

"It's always a good time for a quiz!" 2-Tor said cheerily. "Anatomy. The olfactory glands are used as detectors for which of the five senses?"

Rick adjusted his glasses with a flash of confidence. "2-Tor, this is totally unnecessary. You know that my vast intellect would ace any quiz you put before me. The answer is your sense of smell, by the way."

"We have more important things to deal with right now." Evie left the storage hold and headed for the sanitation room. "Like finding Doctor Grant and building the eighth continent."

Rick followed her. "Evie's right. We have absolutely no time for further quiz questions."

2-Tor beeped in protest. Evie smiled at her brother. "Aw, thanks, Rick. I'm sorry I yelled at you before."

"That's okay," Rick replied. "I may have gone a little overboard on the whole 'it was Evie's fault' thing."

They reached out to hug but quickly recoiled.

"Yeaaugh!" Rick retched. "You smell terrible! Like a wet sneaker filled with moldy turnips."

Evie laughed. "So do you!"

After hot, soapy showers that left the kids feeling clean and refreshed, the Lane children reunited in the *Roost*'s lounge to discuss the next phase of their plan.

"Here's what I found in the database," Rick said, sharing with his sister the notes he'd taken on his phone. "After Dad and Doctor Grant canceled the Eden Compound project, Dad took over as the head of Lane Industries and started a family. Mastercorp assumed that because Doctor Grant was older and the project leader, he must have been the mastermind behind the compound. A big weapons manufacturer like Mastercorp was not about to let all the money they'd spent go to waste, so they pressured Doctor Grant into producing weapons for them."

Evie interrupted, "That's so unfair. How could Mastercorp force Doctor Grant to make weapons?"

"From what I've read, you do not want to cross a company like Mastercorp," Rick said. "Anyway, Winterpole's reports showed that Doctor Grant worked for Mastercorp for a while but hated it and fled the facility at the first opportunity. After that, Winterpole tracked him for several years as he worked on various projects independently. One of the last projects listed in Winterpole's records was an artificial island Doctor Grant was designing. Imagine, a raft the size of an island, with houses and a park and a virtual reality arcade right on top of it! They call it a seastead, like a homestead, but on the sea. I've read about them online."

"It sounds like Dad's teacher was also trying to make an eighth continent. Cool!"

"I even found the coordinates of where Doctor Grant wanted to begin construction in the North Atlantic."

"You know what we need to do?" Evie asked, bouncing like a puppy ready for a walk.

2-Tor snapped his metal beak. "Go home and study and not fall into any danger?"

Evie laughed out loud. "Oh, 2-Tor. You're so cute when you're overprotective."

2-Tor's robotic voice grew quite agitated. "Little Miss, it would betray my programming to behave any other way. It is a wonder you haven't short-circuited me by now."

Evie didn't have the heart to tell 2-Tor that she had tried to do just that many times. "Rick, chart a course for home."

"Oh, I'm so glad you have finally seen reason!" 2-Tor's servos hummed with relief.

Evie giggled. "We're just refueling the *Roost* and then hurrying to the North Atlantic. We've got a scientist to find! Right, Rick?"

Rick gave no reply. His eyes were fixed on the view

window on the port side of the *Roost*, a look of befuddlement on his flushed face.

Running to the window, Evie followed Rick's gaze. Flapping its little mechanical wings, just outside the window, was a pink robo-bird. It was the size of a pigeon, but plated with a hard plastic exoskeleton. The bird wore a gold tiara encrusted with rubies. Its eyes flashed. They were obviously cameras. As Evie reached the window, the camera eyes flashed again, and the bird dove out of view.

The kids ran to the cockpit to check their scanners for signs of the bird, but it was gone. Evie couldn't figure out where the bird had come from. She'd never seen a model like it before. It could have been one of her father's, but if that was the case, why wouldn't the bird have said hello? Why wouldn't Dad have told them he was sending a robo-bird to check on them?

Even if it was possible that her dad had sent the bird, something told Evie it wasn't a Lane design. She could feel it. Someone else had sent the bird, but who, Evie wasn't sure.

Less than a minute later, the *Roost* landed in the front yard of Lane Mansion. Rick and Evie ran up to the entrance, eager to get started on the next part of their adventure and forget about the mysterious bird.

"It's good to have some order for a change," Rick said. "After all the chaos, it looks like we know where we're going next."

Evie opened the front door, revealing the shadowy face of Mister Snow.

"Correct," he said in a dark voice. "You are going to the Prison at the Pole."

10

THE LANE MANSION LIVING ROOM HAD SHRUNK SINCE THE LAST TIME RICK HAD BEEN HOME.

In fact, it had shrunk so much it felt like the walls were closing in on him, tightening like some sort of ancient torture device.

He had never gotten in trouble before. It was always Evie and their dad who got punished for shirking responsibilities and breaking the rules. Rick was all milk and cookies after dinner and an extra hour of TV before bed. What was his mother going to say now? A whole family of delinquents under one roof.

Maybe Rick could pass off his involvement in Evie's scheme as an unwilling accomplice. Play dumb to the fact that she was waging a secret war against Winterpole, one of the most powerful institutions in the world.

But who would believe that lie? Kid genius Rick Lane, play dumb? Never.

As they sat on the sofa, it became clear that Evie had no clue how hot the water they were in was. While Dad struggled to scratch an itch under his squid-cuff, she was talking Mister Snow's ear off about injustice and the unassailable character of their bird-thief father.

"You have no right to punish us!" Evie shouted. "There's no crime in trying to free your father. We've done nothing wrong."

Except the Winterpole inspector *did* have the right to penalize trespassers, hackers, and spies. All of which Rick and Evie were. So technically, according to Rick's calculations, they had done fourteen or fifteen things wrong.

Mister Snow took a sip of their mother's favorite tea. He had said, "Sorry, miss, just doing my job," so many times he had given up on it, and now he pursed his lips and stared into his teacup without a sound.

For over an hour, that was how they sat, with Rick panicking about his fate, Evie protesting the system, and Mister Snow generating enough kinetic energy with his pursed lips to power a small battery.

The Winterpole officer jumped out of his chair when his pocket buzzed. He pulled out his flip phone and answered the call. "Agent Snow here. Yes. Yes. What?! But, Director, I—no! Hrrr . . . yes, Director. I understand." He closed his phone with a defiant snap.

"You really don't need to punish my children," Rick's father explained to the Winterpole agent. "I will make sure they are severely scolded."

"I am afraid that will not suffice," Mister Snow said. "However, Headquarters has just informed me that because your children are minors, we cannot penalize them as I would like. So, alas, Evelyn and Richard will not be visiting the prison at this time. Shame." Mister Snow paused for a moment, as if taking in this devastating news once more. Then his face brightened. "But you are their guardian, and your crimes are already well documented, and you are not a minor—although your behavior sometimes leaves me wondering—so we will be adding to your punishments on behalf of your children."

"What? No!" Evie exclaimed.

"You can't do that," Rick said forcefully.

Mister Snow ignored them. "Consider this your final warning, Mister Lane. I have activated the electromagnetic-pulse function on your squid-cuff and set it to a two-foot radius. Like all EMPs, this one will fry any electronic devices it comes in contact with. No computers. No electricity. No outside communication."

"No video games?" Rick asked, horrified.

Mister Snow's eyes narrowed as he regarded Rick's father. "If you or your children make any attempt to contact Doctor Evan Grant, we will not hesitate to send you to the Prison at the Pole." The inspector finally glanced in Rick and Evie's direction. "This is for their own good. And besides, I don't even think that dangerous man is alive anymore."

Rick abhorred violence, but he had half a mind to take a swing at Mister Snow. He stayed his hand, knowing it would only get his father in more trouble. "Now that you have ended our search and trapped my dad, are you going to call off that robo-bird you have following us around?"

"What are you talking about?" Mister Snow asked. "That big robot who flies your tree is *your* bird."

"Not 2-Tor, the other one. The little pink one we saw spying on us."

"I have never heard of such a device. Perhaps you imagined it, the way you imagined that I would not catch you. I always will, Richard Lane. Remember that." The Lanes walked Mister Snow to the door as he continued to berate them. "Do as you're told, or you'll be out in the cold," he snickered, amused with himself. "Hey! That kind of rhymed!"

They shut the front door behind Mister Snow as he hurried to his hovership, leaving Rick and Evie standing as close to their father as they could in a show of support. Unfortunately, "as close as they could" meant that they were actually more than two feet away. Any closer and his squid-cuff would destroy their cell phones.

11

MISSION FAILURE, EVIE THOUGHT, WATCHING FROM THE LIVING ROOM WINDOWS AS MISTER SNOW'S hovership disappeared into the clouds. Winterpole was too powerful, and now the risks were too great. Even she, who had sworn she would not rest until she stood on the solid earth of the eighth continent, had no options left. If she kept up her quest, her father would surely be sent to the Prison at the Pole. As it was, he had already sacrificed so much—his freedom, his inventions, everything.

She moved to give him a comforting hug, but he backed away.

"Wait, wait! Don't come any closer," he said urgently. "The EMP!"

The cockatoo perched on a bookshelf nearby screeched in frustration on its owner's behalf. The cacophony filled Evie's ears. Rick expressed his feelings in the opposite way, pushing his chin against his chest and brooding quietly.

"Kids, listen to me." Dad knelt down so they were all at eye level. "You can't worry about the risks, not now, after you have already come so far. No matter what happens to me, you must continue your search. You must find Doctor Grant and build the eighth continent. It's the only hope we have of getting out of this mess."

"We think we know where he is," Evie said. "He's apparently building an island in the Arctic Circle."

Clapping his hands with amusement, her father said, "Ha! Evan, you dog. Of course he is. Great minds, after all. This is the good news we needed. Come with me down to my lab. I have something to show you both."

The front door opened, and 2-Tor poked his silver domed head through, carrying a tower of wildly colored suitcases between his wings. "Doctor Lane! I have urgent news to convey to you."

"It's all right, 2-Tor," Evie's father assured the robot. "Rick and Evie have told me everything."

2-Tor wailed, "No! You don't understand. It's much worse than any of our setbacks."

The frantic tone in the robot's voice worried Evie. "What is it, 2-Tor? What's wrong?"

"It's dreadful, just dreadful news."

"Did Winterpole come back?" asked Rick.

"Is the *Roost* broken again?" asked Evie.

"No!" 2-Tor lamented. "It's your mother, children. Madam Lane has returned from her business trip."

Evie's father looked at 2-Tor, then at the luggage he was holding. Mom's luggage. Dad's eyes went as wide as optical discs. "Kids, you have to hide me, quick! She can't see me with this stupid squid around my leg."

"See you?" Rick repeated. "You mean you still haven't told her about the arrest or the Eden Compound . . . or any of this stuff? I don't believe it. At this rate, there isn't going to be anything left of Lane Industries when we grow up."

"In all of our phone talks the opportunity never arose."

Rick gritted his teeth. "'Never arose'?! How does getting arrested and being imprisoned in your own house never arose?"

"Never arise," Evie corrected.

"Quiet, Evie," Rick snapped, shoving his sister.

"Hey, knock it off!" Their father's cheeks reddened. "The truth is, I was waiting for the right moment."

"We can fight about this later," Evie replied, displaying an amount of grace that surprised even herself. "Right now, we need to sneak Dad down to his workshop and look for a way to conceal his squid-cuff. If Mom finds out what we've been up to, we'll *wish* we'd been sent to the Prison at the Pole."

It wasn't that Mom was terrible. She was the best Frisbee thrower Evie had ever seen, she could ski like a pro, and she used to read them the greatest bedtime stories—each one was like a performance. But as the CEO of Cleanaspot, the world's third-largest international soap manufacturer, she was also a mega-powerful businesswoman. These days, she was always traveling and working. Just last week she was in Dubai consulting with hotel magnates about how to improve laundry procedures. After solving the problem of the sheikh's sheets, she was off to Prague for the European Bubble Festival, of which Cleanaspot was a major sponsor.

Evie, Rick, their dad, and 2-Tor crept down the stairs, careful not to make a sound. Every time 2-Tor's joints squeaked, Evie winced, and she wished she had actually listened all those times her dad had told her to clean him.

Through the ceiling, they heard Mom's voice giving her cell phone a stern lecture. "Catherine, for the last time, this is UN-AC-CEPTABLE. I want those sud reports on my desk by Monday morning, or we are all going out with the wash. Is that understood? . . . Good. Have a great weekend."

They heard Mom walk into the kitchen, and so they sped back up the stairs and into the front hall, where she had just been.

"Quick, hide me!" The kids' father ran to the hall closet and opened the door. Four wetsuits, a surfboard, and two fifty-pound bags of birdseed tumbled onto the floor.

Evie's mom burst into the room. "George! What are you doing?"

Evie's dad pulled his foot under the bags of birdseed to conceal the squid-cuff. "Melinda! Hi! Welcome home! Nothing! Just helping the kids clean out the closet."

She glanced at Rick and Evie briefly before returning her attention to their dad. "Hi, kids. George, we have that dinner at the International Lodge with those investors from the Soap Syndicate in forty minutes. Why aren't you dressed?"

"Oh! Um . . ."

"Did you forget?"

Evie's father swallowed hard. "No, uh, of course not! Just lost track of the time."

"Well, hurry up! I'm going to shower. We are leaving in ten minutes." She hurried up the stairs.

Rick, Evie, and their dad exhaled a collective sigh of relief.

They scrambled down to the workshop, where on the flatscreen Geneva's 110th annual bon bon–eating competition was playing. Evie's dad kept clear of the television so that he wouldn't torch it with his squid-cuff. "Rick," he said, "run over to my laptop. Pull up the file 'EC Zero to Zero-Point-Five' and transfer it to your portable hard drive."

"You got it, Dad."

Suddenly, Mom's face appeared on the TV screen. Her hair was wet, and she was in a towel. A foamy toothbrush hung out of her mouth. In a panic, Evie's dad stuck his foot in a tool chest.

"George!" Evie's mom said around the toothbrush. "What are you doing down there?"

"Sorry, honey! Just showing the kids a new video game I developed!"

"We don't have time for that! This is UN-AC-CEPTABLE. Go put on your suit."

Evie's father looked nervous. "Sure thing, honey! Just a minute."

The image on the screen went back to people stuffing their faces with chocolates.

Minutes passed as Rick worked out how to transfer the file their dad had sent him to find. Evie paced, agitated.

Their dad stood perfectly still in the middle of the room, trying not to get too close to his computer equipment or any other electronics in the workshop.

"Got it," Rick said at last, raising his portable hard drive like the triumphant knight raising his sword in *The Saga of Salma*. "What is it?"

"That's my half of the Eden Compound," their dad explained. "When you find Doctor Grant, he should be able to reassemble the formula using his half. Hopefully, he can make enough of the compound to create the eighth continent."

Evie's mom burst into the room. She looked ravishing, wearing a flowing emerald ball gown that matched the earrings she was struggling to fit through her ears. In the second it took Evie to look at her, her dad had thrown a greasy white sheet over himself like a blanket, once again hiding the squid-cuff.

"George!" Evie's mother said. "We are going to be so late."

"Cough! Cough! Oh, Melinda. I don't think I can go. I think I ate some bad, uh"—he glanced at the television—"bonbons yesterday, and I feel like a goat cheese salad left out in the sun. I don't think I can do anything tonight."

"Oh, you poor dear!" She stepped toward him to feel the temperature of his forehead with her hand.

"No, Melinda! Wait!" Her husband tried to stop her, but it was too late. She entered the EMP's invisible two-foot radius, and her cell phone exploded, blowing a hole in her purse. Lip gloss, old receipts, and her pocketbook tumbled to the floor.

"What on earth?" she asked, the wrinkles on her forehead at full attention. "My phone! Oh, dear. Maybe this is a sign I shouldn't attend the banquet."

"No, go!" George insisted desperately. "I'm okay. It's an important meeting. I'll put myself to bed."

"I don't know, sweetie. Are you sure?"

Evie took a closer look at her father. The edge of the squid-cuff had begun to peek out from the bottom corner of his blanket. "Yup, definitely sure," he said.

"Oh, uh, okay, if that's what you want." Evie's mother headed to the door, then hesitated. "I'll get you some chicken soup before I leave. Feel better, honey. Have a good night, kids."

"Bye, Mom!" Rick and Evie chorused.

When she was gone, Rick turned to Evie. "We need to fess up to Mom. This whole thing is a bad idea. Maybe we should just give up on the eighth continent. Maybe it's not worth it."

"Maybe you need to pull yourself together," Evie snapped at him. "Think of all the trouble you've already gotten into. You want that to be for nothing? Winterpole is using Dad to keep us in line. Don't think they won't make note of what we did on your permanent record."

Rick gasped. "Einstein's ghost! My permanent record? I almost forgot about that. Evie, what are we going to do?"

"We are going to build the eighth continent. That's the only way we can keep Dad from going to the Prison at the Pole. He stole that bird. We broke into Winterpole Headquarters and hacked their data system. We tampered with their records. Well, I tampered with their records. But we can't turn back now. We have to build the eighth continent, and we can't let Mom find out about it."

Rick had the most horrified expression on his face, like a grotesque statue in a haunted house.

Evie shoved him. "It's not that bad. We'll be fine."

But Rick wasn't looking at Evie. He was looking over her shoulder, where their mother was standing in the doorway, her head steaming even more than the bowl of chicken soup in her hands.

12

MRS. MAPLE'S OFFICE WAS THE EPITOME OF MODERN DESIGN AND CONTAINED ALL THE THINGS a precise woman like Diana's mother desired. A fine Swiss cuckoo clock adorned each wall, and a tremendous model of Winterpole Headquarters, carved of crystal clear ice, dominated the center of the room.

Mrs. Maple had several important meetings to attend that day, which left Diana and Vesuvia alone to do their homework.

"And so," Diana said, finishing up an algebra problem, "if you divide both sides by two, you're left with just x on this side, and six over here. X equals six. See?"

Vesuvia flipped her tablet onto the coffee table. It bounced off and landed on the floor. She stretched like a cheetah after a big meal. "Uggggchh! My brain is exhausted from listening to you. Thank polyester I'm done with math."

Diana scratched the back of her head awkwardly. "Heh-heh. Yeah. Um, Vesuvia? Now that I've finished your homework, do you think I could get started on mine?"

"I have a better idea," Vesuvia said, swiping the tablet

from Diana's hand and flinging it into the ice sculpture, where it struck with a wet *crack!* "Let's play Bribe Your Mom's Coworkers for Information about the Lanes."

"That's a long name for a game," Diana observed.

"Don't be a know-it-all, Diana. They're ugly. Now, we still don't know how the Lanes intend to make the eighth continent, and without that information I can't build New Miami."

Vesuvia was right. Diana had not seen Rick and Evie since they rode by her mother's office window two days earlier. Since then, Vesuvia had embedded herself at Winterpole Headquarters, scouring the facility for any information that would provide answers about the Lanes' plan for the eighth continent. Now the weekend was almost over, and they were still no closer to solving the puzzle.

"Come on, Diana!" Vesuvia nudged her. "We need to know what they were looking for when they snuck in here."

Diana shrugged. "I guess I could ask my mom for permission."

"Sigh!" Vesuvia heaved aloud. "My way is much more fun. Who doesn't like to get paid to *not* do something? Daddy pays me fifty thousand US dollars a month *not* to drown my new puppy in the kitchen sink. It's awesome! And the joke's on Daddy, because I don't even *want* to do that again. After the first time, what's the point?"

Diana wanted to be horrified by this statement, but she had been friends with Vesuvia long enough to expect such twisted things to come from her mouth.

"Come on. Let's go!" Vesuvia hopped up, brimming with excitement. "Carry my tablet."

Diana picked it up. A few glass shards fell out of the screen. She showed Vesuvia the spiderweb of cracks. "I think it's broken."

Vesuvia groaned. "Be sure to file an official complaint. They put no effort into making those things last. All the time they break for no reason. Now. Onward! To the Bribe Zone!"

Diana had suggested that they begin their search at the guard barracks, where the uniformed troops who patrolled the halls of Winterpole Headquarters hung out when they weren't on duty. Winterpole guards gossiped like, well, like anyone with a watercooler or an Internet connection, to be honest. It was possible that one of them knew something about Rick and Evie's plan.

The drab barracks housed two rows of long blue cots, like the kind Diana used to take naps on in preschool. There was a small kitchen with no stove and a refrigerator filled with nothing but ice water. At the end of the room two guards were sitting in undershirts and sweatpants, hunched over a wet piece of tile floor. They were throwing ice dice, carved with a toothpick to indicate the dots on each face.

"Hurry up, Larry. Throw before the dice melt."

Larry cupped the ice dice and blew hard on them. "It serves no purpose to roll, Barry, if I have not successfully channeled my luck."

"Well, don't blow on them. You will only make them melt faster."

With a flick of his wrist, Larry tossed the dice. They tumbled across the floor, settling on the numbers five and six.

"No, no, no!" Barry wailed.

"Yes, yes, yes! Eleven!" Larry cheered.

Vesuvia put her foot down. Literally. The ice dice went *crunch* under her pink patent pleather pumps. "What are you two idiots doing? Gambling, on Winterpole property? What would the director say about this appalling display?"

Barry mumbled, "Statute CS-Ta states that on our downtime we must relax however we choose."

"One time I received a penalty for failing to observe mandatory recreation hours," Larry added.

"I am appalled," Vesuvia sniffed in loathing. "Now, you listen to me and do as I tell you, or you are both going to be in hot water."

Barry shivered involuntarily. "Well, technically most of the water around Winterpole is fairly cold."

"Silence!" Vesuvia hissed. "You are going to tell me everything you know about Rick and Evie Lane."

A soft but stern voice behind them spoke. "They are not authorized to divulge that information—even if they did know it."

Diana turned to see Mister Snow in a trim suit peering down at her. Mister Snow had never been one of Diana's favorite agents. Far from it. He never treated her special the way many did. He really stuck to the letter of the statutes, a true believer in Winterpole's mission. It obviously wasn't just a job to him.

Mister Snow met her eyes and looked perplexed. "Diana, what are you doing here?"

"We can go wherever we want," Vesuvia snapped. "But

now that you're here, maybe you can take us someplace else."

"It is against regulations for me to take you to unauthorized locations in the building." He led them back into the hall. "Why? Where would you like to go?"

"Take us to the computer room where Rick and Evie Lane hacked your system."

"Whoa!" Mister Snow held up his hands in surprise. "That's awfully nosy of you."

Vesuvia snarled like a rabid poodle.

"Don't make fun of her nose," Diana cautioned. "She hates that."

"All Winterpole business with the Lane family has been discarded. We no longer recognize them as a legal entity. And besides, the computer room in question is taped off for an investigation. Statute 20-51 prohibits me from showing you taped-off areas."

"But what about Statute 100?" Vesuvia asked, slipping out of her purse a note for 100 Swiss francs.

Confused, Mister Snow asked, "Only authorized personnel are certified to refill watercoolers?" Then he glared at her. "Oh, wait a second. Young lady, are you trying to bribe me?"

Undeterred, Vesuvia reached for another bill. "Statute 105?"

The inspector turned to Diana. "Listen, I don't care who this girl thinks she is, or whose daughter you are, but what she is doing violates a half-dozen regulations."

Vesuvia stuffed the money back into her purse. "Fine. We'll ask someone else."

"You can ask the curb," Mister Snow said.

Vesuvia put her hands on her hips. "The who?"

13

THE CONCRETE CURB RUSHED UP AND STRUCK DIANA IN THE EVERYWHERE. SHE HAD UNDERSTOOD THE metaphor but had not expected Mister Snow to literally throw them out of Winterpole Headquarters.

"Vesuvia, are you all right?" Diana asked. She had seen her friend land on her head.

"No. I am not all right. I am in the worst imaginable pain."

Diana scrambled over to Vesuvia and began checking her for broken bones. "Oh my goodness. What's wrong?"

"My beautiful haircut," Vesuvia wailed. "Look at it. I have a split end!" The little CEO pulled her pink plastic jacket over her head and wept. "I can't believe this! No one has ever treated me with such disrespect. I am outraged!"

Diana sighed. She should have known better than to worry. Vesuvia's skull was harder than a robot's. Instead, she focused her concerns on what her mother would say when she found out Mister Snow had thrown them out of her office. She would probably freak out about such a blemish on her spotless record. It was always about how things affected *her*. Maybe that was why it was surprisingly easy for Diana to get along with Vesuvia. Experience.

Her friend continued her rant. "I am going to call Bradley and make sure this Mister Snowflake is banned from all Condo Corp properties."

Diana pushed her thoughts from her mind and focused on the matter at hand. How were they going to figure out what the Lanes were up to?

"Bradley? I am hopping mad. No—a hop is too little. I am leaping mad. Pole-vaulting mad. I am . . . What? The board met without me? Get Billingsley on the phone right now!"

Something caught Diana's eye. Out in the parking lot, a big green Dumpster gleamed in the afternoon sunlight like an emerald on the asphalt. She remembered the words that Mister Snow had said back inside Winterpole Headquarters. That all information pertaining to the Lane family had been "discarded." Would Winterpole be dumb enough to simply "discard" the Lane family file in a public Dumpster?

Vesuvia screamed into her phone. "Winterpole is so stupid you could use its head as a flotation device. . . . Well, I know organizations don't have heads. They have leaders but not heads like I meant. Literal heads. Shut up, Bradley. You know what I mean."

Diana figured they *would* be dumb enough—or at least beholden to some fifty-year-old rule that all documents must be discarded in the public Dumpster. While Vesuvia verbally abused her telephone, Diana crossed the parking lot and peered into the trash.

She returned to the curb a moment later with a stack of documents bound with a couple of rubber bands. The papers were a little crumpled and bespeckled with coffee grounds. Still, their sheer existence made Diana quite happy.

"I cannot *believe* he had the nerve to throw me out. No one throws Vesuvia Piffle anything! Except perhaps a party, with little pink cupcakes and a cotton candy machine and one of those bouncy castles."

"Hey, Vesuvia, look at this." Diana hefted the big stack of papers.

"You're right," Vesuvia said into her phone. "That is an excellent idea. I'd like pink strawberry cotton candy. And don't get me a bouncy castle that looks like a castle. I want a double bouncy castle, shaped like New Miami!"

"Vesuvia!" With each failed conversation, it took less time before Diana started shouting. "This is very important! It's about the Lanes."

"Money? I'm not paying for a stupid cotton candy machine. Call Daddy. He takes care of all that boring stuff."

Diana hurled the stack of papers in Vesuvia's direction. "Here, catch!"

The stack of papers struck Vesuvia in the chest and knocked her onto her butt, sending her phone spinning in a little circle on the ground beside her. Diana held her breath, waiting for the inevitable Vesuvia eruption, but none came, because now that Vesuvia was sitting, she couldn't help but look at the papers, which had landed in her lap. The cover sheet read: *Lane Enterprises, George Lane, Family & Associates.*

"This is amazing!" Vesuvia hugged the stack of papers in pure jubilation.

"I know!" Diana grinned triumphantly.

"Where did you find this?"

"Can you believe it? In the trash."

Vesuvia's smile melted into pure horror. She shrieked so loudly Diana had to cover her ears. "EEEEEEEEEEEEEEEEE! Grossest! Nastiest! Boil my hands! YUCK! EW! THE GARBAGE!" She kicked the papers from her lap and crawled away.

"Just look at it, Vesuvia."

"It was in the garbage, Diana. I hate garbage! How could you give that to me?" She fanned out her clothes and stomped her feet and spun around in a circle, shaking away the germs.

Diana pressed the issue. "You have to look at it. It's important. It's the information you were looking for about the Lanes."

"What?!" Vesuvia spun on her heel and snatched the stack of papers from Diana's hand. "Give that to me!" She ripped off the rubber bands with a snap and flipped through the pages, Diana reading over her shoulder. The papers detailed the incident in the computer room and an outline of the information that Rick and Evie Lane had gathered there. There were several references to a Doctor Evan Grant, a former colleague of the Lanes' father. Apparently he had developed a chemical substance called the Eden Compound, which converted trash into dirt and other organic materials.

Vesuvia snorted and began to crumple up the paper. "Boring. It's just some nerdy science stuff."

"Vesuvia, wait!" Diana smoothed out the paper. "Look. This Doctor Grant must be who the Lanes are looking for. With this Eden Compound, Rick and Evie could transform the Great Pacific Garbage Patch into a real island. That's how they're going to build their eighth continent. I can't believe it."

"I know!" Vesuvia said. "I can't believe they thought they would ever build the continent. It's obvious that I am going to kidnap this doctor man and force him to make New Miami on Trash Island. Then the eighth continent will be mine!"

"No, I mean I can't believe Winterpole just left this information in the garbage Dumpster."

A look of recognition dawned on Vesuvia's face. She was still holding the stack of papers, the stack of papers that until just a few moments ago had been in the trash. Her face wrenched up in disgust, her screams setting off half the car alarms in the parking lot.

14

THE SHORT GRASS FELT SOFT BETWEEN EVIE'S TOES, LIKE A SPONGY CARPET. THE SUN WARMED the top of her head, and she inhaled the ocean breeze. There was nothing quite like going for a walk on your own continent.

The untapped, beautiful land filled her with joy and triumph. This was her continent. She had built it. No one could take that accomplishment, or this land, away from her.

"Evie! Eeeeeeeevieeeeeeeee! Come play with us!"

She turned to the sound of the voice. Her father was waving at her from across the green field. Her mother and Rick were doing cartwheels and blowing dandelions and climbing trees. What fun!

Her sprint across the field took no time at all. She leaped into her father's arms, and he spun her, and they laughed.

"I am so proud of you, my darling." His smile was as warm as the sun. "I knew you could do it."

"I built a kingdom!" she giggled. It felt so good to have given the world a place as tranquil and trash-free as the eighth continent. But really, she was happy to have a safe haven where she was the boss, where Winterpole and her wicked schoolmates were not allowed.

Evie stood on her tiptoes to give her dad a kiss on the nose, but she stopped short.

"What is it, honey?" her father asked.

Something oozed from her father's nostril. Blood? No. It was black ichor, and when it touched his lips it stained them dark, and he gagged.

"Dad! Something's wrong."

"I don't feel well." Her father stumbled and dropped to his knees. "Evie, help me!"

"I don't know what to do!"

"You never did know anything. You're useless," he said with hate in his eyes. And then he transformed into a Dad-shaped pile of garbage.

New waves of trash surged from the pile until it was the size of a house, a monstrous beast with broken televisions for eyes, teeth of rusted sheet metal, and rotten food for hands. It enveloped her mom and brother with one swipe.

Then the monster went for her. It had her mother's face, and when its mouth closed around Evie's head, she screamed.

She was still screaming when she snapped awake in her bed from the horrible nightmare.

Evie combed damp hair from her face, gasping for breath. Her favorite pajamas were soaked with sweat.

She got out of bed, put on a clean T-shirt, and crept

downstairs to the kitchen. She needed water or a cup of milk. Something to get the taste of garbage out of her mouth.

The light was on in the kitchen. She entered cautiously. The dark marble countertops were spotless. The stainless steel saucepans, hanging from the ceiling like chandeliers, were even more stainless than usual.

"Oh. Evelyn. I didn't see you there."

Evie jumped at the voice, still a little shaken from the awful dream, then searched for its source. Her mother was on the floor, scrubbing the tiles with her gloves, which were covered with little bristles, like hand-shaped toothbrushes.

"Sorry, Mom. I just wanted some water."

Her mother stood and took off the gloves. "Let me get it for you." She poured the water through Dad's homemade quintuple-filtration system. When Evie drank it, the water tasted cleaner than any she'd ever sipped.

Melinda watched as her daughter drained her glass. "Bad dream?"

"How did you know?"

"When you were a baby, your ears would get red whenever you had a nightmare. And right now your ears are stop signs."

Evie covered her ears, embarrassed.

"Oh, don't do that. They're beautiful." She tucked a lock of hair behind Evie's right ear. "Do you want to talk about it?"

Evie shook her head. "Are you still mad about Dad and the eighth continent and everything?"

Her mother sighed. "Yes, I'm still mad."

A few days ago, when her mother had found out about the family's attempt to create their own continent, no questions were needed to determine her feelings. Rick and Evie had been grounded so quick they got whiplash. Mom shared her fury with everyone. With Dad for breaking Winterpole's rules, with Evie for her crazy continent-building scheme, even with Rick, whom she was never angry at, for going along with them. "I can't believe you kids are following in your father's footsteps," she had said. "Well, at least I can't believe *Richard* is following in his footsteps. Evelyn's behavior isn't terribly surprising." The only member of the Lane family she wasn't mad at was 2-Tor, whose programming prevented him from lying, and so he had spilled the birdseed about everything that had happened.

But now things seemed . . . okay. Evie downed the final drops of water as her mother said, "I've always loved your father for his vision. I wanted the world clean. He wanted it free of trash. It was the same dream. Our methods, by contrast, could not be more different. You learn to accept the people you love for who they are, even if they make you crazy."

Evie nodded. "Rick is so timid it drives me nuts."

"And you're so brazen it drives *him* nuts. But you still love each other."

"Mom . . ." Evie hesitated. She had a question that required an answer, but she was afraid to ask in case it made her mother even angrier.

"What is it, honey?"

Deep breath. "You always seem so disappointed in me, but you never get that way with Rick. How come? Is it because I'm always getting in trouble, and you don't see any of yourself in me?"

Her mother sighed. "First of all, Rick's good behavior mystifies me too. Sometimes I wonder if the hospital didn't give us a well-behaved robot by mistake. As for your question, quite the opposite is true. I see so much of myself in you that whenever you talk I remember all the crazy stuff I did when I was your age, but my heart aches at the same time. You just don't have the experience I do. You don't understand what it means to be focused and have ambitions. I want you to make something of yourself, honey, but you are never going to do that if you're running around all the time on these silly adventures away from school."

Evie thought, but did not say, that her adventures were anything but silly. Her adventures were how she wanted to make something of herself. Her mother really didn't get it. Evie was not going to grow up and sit behind a desk all day; she was going to stay a kid and make the world a cleaner, awesomer place. She wished she could find a way to show her mom how important the eighth continent was. Maybe then she would understand.

They sat silently in the kitchen for a long time. At last, her mother said, "Do you know why I like clean things? It's because you can see things for what they are. Clean things can't hide behind dirt or in garbage. When something is clean, it has no secrets. Your father is different. He thinks mess fosters ingenuity. I guess that's a fancy way of saying that when you're messy, sometimes you make happy accidents. But sometimes you make very bad accidents, like when you sneak into an international security agency and tamper with their official documents."

"So I guess I'm still grounded," Evie said sourly.

"Most certainly." Her mother nodded, her lips hinting at a smile. "And Richard too. I'm sure someday he will find a way to cope, but I think it's good for him to stew for now. Builds character."

Evie snickered. "He almost fainted."

Her mother's mouth crinkled into a smile. "Listen, honey. I'm off in the morning to a very important meeting about the future of Cleanaspot."

"Where is it?"

"Barbados."

"Barbados is nice."

"I agree." Her mother put an arm around Evie's shoulder. "But what would also be nice is if you could please behave while I'm gone."

Evie looked away.

"Please, Evie, for me." She gently squeezed her daughter's chin. "And do try to keep your father out of trouble."

Evie nodded.

"Promise?"

"I promise," she answered. But secretly, she could not help but think that the best way to help her father, and make something of herself, was to build the eighth continent.

15

THE NEXT MORNING RICK AND EVIE WOKE UP EARLY TO SEE THEIR MOTHER OFF ON HER BUSINESS

trip. "Remember," she told them before she left, "the best way to keep on the right side of Winterpole is to behave. Don't worry. They will free your father soon enough, as long as you don't do anything else to upset them."

Mom's hovership blasted into the air and flew out of sight. Rick kicked a pebble down the asphalt driveway. His mother was off to Barbados, while he was stuck here, grounded. Rick had never been grounded in his life. It felt worse than when he melted the hard drive with his grammar homework. His father seemed bored with him, and now his mother thought him no better behaved than Evie. Everything was in jeopardy—his family, Lane Industries, his permanent record, and the eighth continent. Meanwhile, he had to get Dad out of that EMP-equipped squid-cuff before he blew up all the video games in the house.

A window on the fourth floor slid open, revealing his father perched on the sill. Dad had been careful to avoid all technology, and the lack of mechanical contact was making him act kind of funny. Now he needed their house helper robot to do everything for him—from a safe distance, of course. The computer was off-limits. He couldn't use the TV remote. He had gotten careless and tried to make himself a bologna sandwich (no crusts) and blew up the refrigerator when he opened it. Now they were all drinking warm soda pop, and Dad was still hungry.

"Kids!" he called from the window. "Hey! Come up here."

Rick's parents' bedroom was the only place where Dad was safe from his squid-cuff's EMP. Mom had a strict no-screens-in-bed rule, so there was nothing in the room to explode.

When Rick, Evie, and 2-Tor entered, they found their father still in his pajamas—a flannel shirt and pants with toucans on them. He paced the floor in agitation, wearing a hole in the soft carpet.

"I've been thinking about your mission." When he spoke, it was in abrupt spurts, each phrase like a little arc of electricity. "You've been home for too long. You must continue your quest to make the eighth continent."

Sometimes Rick felt like Mom Junior talking to his dad. "Don't you ever listen? Mom said we had to give up our quest, for our safety and so you won't get taken away. Think of what would happen to Lane Industries if you're sent to prison. Everything you've built would disappear."

"Never mind that," he said. "I'll worry about your mother. You just worry about finding Doctor Grant."

"'Never mind that'?" Rick wondered how someone so dense could be related to him. "What on earth could be more important than *that*?"

2-Tor squawked in displeasure. This was not a turn of events that Mom would be happy to hear about.

Such a fact didn't seem to deter Rick's father, however. "Son, do you still have my half of the formula that I gave you?" he asked.

On reflex Rick placed his hand on the portable drive in his pocket. His father had entrusted him with his half of the Eden Compound—the family legacy.

"Rick, I know you think I'm crazy, but this risk is worth it. You want to save the family and protect the company. That's what I want too. But you can't go back. We have to go forward, and the eighth continent is right in front of us. The continent is the solution. Keep that hard drive safe. When you find Evan, combining both halves of the formula will be the only way you can create the Eden Compound."

"What if we can't find him?" Rick asked, worried. "What if the Eden Compound doesn't work? What if . . . what if we fail?"

"We won't," Evie said emphatically. "We can't."

Her father flashed her a proud smile. "I love you, my darlings. I wish I could hug you."

Evie took off her backpack, which contained her tablet. Then she took her phone out of her pocket and gave it to Rick. After making sure she had removed every last bit of technology from her body, she rushed into her father's open arms.

George gave her a big squeeze. "Take care of your brother,"

he said. "If he worries too much, he'll get warts."

"I heard that," Rick said, feeling a little left out.

"Shhh . . ." their father hushed. "My bright, brave brood. You can accomplish anything if you believe in yourselves and trust each other."

Evie sniffed, not even trying to hide the tears that were creeping up on her.

"Goodbye, sir!" 2-Tor said, blubbering with virtual emotion. He stomped toward Dad with open wings.

Evie screamed, "2-Tor! No! Wait!"

But it was too late. 2-Tor entered the anti-tech bubble, and the EMP reacted with such force that it blasted 2-Tor across the room. Rick's dad dropped to his knees in pain.

Sparks flew out of 2-Tor's amber eyes. Acrid smoke poured from his beak.

Rick ran to the robot's side and grabbed him, but his metal casing was hot to the touch and burned Rick's hand. "Ow!" he winced. "2-Tor! Are you okay?"

The robot's reply was stiff. "Good morning, Richard. It is time for a quiz."

"No, it's not. It's time to get up." He helped the birdbot to his feet.

"You must leave quickly," his father grunted. "We are getting careless, and there is no time to lose."

"2-Tor can't go like this." Evie gestured toward the smoldering robot.

Rick agreed. "Evie's right, Dad. And Evie's never right."

"Yeah!" Evie said, then, "Wait a minute."

"No debates. Get that bird on the *Roost* and get out of here!"

16

THE *ROOST* FLEW FROM GENEVA HEADING NORTH BY NORTHWEST, OVER FRANCE, THE ENGLISH

Channel, and the handsome city of London, then high-fived Ireland and cut over the North Atlantic toward Greenland. 2-Tor navigated, while Rick manned the controls. Evie would never admit it to her brother, but Rick was an exceptional pilot.

Seeing the world from this height left Evie feeling frustrated. Every beach wore a necklace of accumulated garbage—sewage and seaweed and scuttlebutt, all scrambled together. She did not have to look hard to see signs of trash choking the environment.

Evie needed something to take her mind off it. She turned to Rick. "What do you think Doctor Grant is going to say when we tell him that we're Dad's kids, and we want to make a new continent with their old formula? I bet he's going to be super surprised and super excited to change the world."

Rick shrugged. "I dunno, Evie. The guy has been at sea for a long time, assuming he is even still there. He went into

111

hiding years ago. Maybe he left the ocean years ago too."

"But then he could be anywhere!" Evie slapped her forehead. "Oh no . . ."

"Don't worry. I'm sure that if he's gone, there will be at least some clue to help us find our way to him. Besides, maybe he finished building the seastead, and he'll give us a grand tour!"

Evie hoped that was true. Imagine, an entire city floating on the water. Perhaps some modern-day pioneers had already moved into the houses built alongside the artificial roads. Maybe entrepreneurial families had already established ordinary lives there. Something Evie's father had taught her was that progress doesn't really happen until something extraordinary becomes normal. All the great scientific breakthroughs of the previous century were terrifying when they were first presented. Cars, airplanes, the Internet. When social robots hit the market, people thought there would be an uprising and machine overlords would enslave them. But that was just ignorant fear. Maybe human beings would enslave each other if they had the means and the will to do it, but robots would never be so cruel. It was the same with her father's inventions. When he first displayed his hovership technology, the only thing anyone talked about was the danger. But he had proven them all wrong. Now those same protesters could not imagine life without a speedy hover engine.

Rick grabbed Evie's arm, distracting her from her thoughts. "We're flying over Iceland now. Look!"

"Wow!" Evie said, peering out the window at the fields

below, trying to orient herself. "It's so green!"

"Haha. Yup! Iceland is green, and Greenland is ice."

"How come?"

"Children," 2-Tor interrupted, "your parents have instructed me to issue you a quiz at certain times in your travels, so that you remain academically efficient."

Evie rolled her eyes. "Yeah, 2-Tor, we know. You quiz us all the time."

2-Tor apparently wasn't dissuaded. "It is time for a quiz," he said. "Testing initiated."

"Oh, here we go." Evie rolled her eyes. "This should be fun."

"It is fun," Rick said, "assuming you study and know the answers."

"Children," 2-Tor growled like an overworked refrigerator, "your parents have instructed me to issue you a quiz at certain times in your travels, so that you remain academically efficient. It is time for a quiz. Testing initiated."

Rick and Evie exchanged a worried look. This was not normal.

"Uh . . . yeah, 2-Tor," Evie said. "You just mentioned that."

"Quiz time!" 2-Tor said. "Geography. True or false, Erik the Red discovered Greenland in the year 983."

Rick started to speak when Evie cut him off. She wanted to give a correct answer for once.

"True!"

"*Bzzzzt!*" 2-Tor flapped his wings in irritation. "False. Erik the Red discovered Greenland in the year 982."

Rick groaned. "Come on, Evie. I knew that one."

"Mythology. What Arctic sea creature was wrongly thought to be the mythical unicorn?"

"Narwhal!" Rick cheered.

"False!" 2-Tor spat. "The answer is the kangaroo."

Rick glared. "That's wrong, 2-Tor. Kangaroos come from Australia, not the North Pole."

"Incorrect," 2-Tor spat back. "The correct answer is hydrogen-hydrogen-oxygen. More commonly known as H_2O."

Evie clung to her brother's arm. "Ricky . . . 2-Tor is scaring me."

2-Tor spread his wings. One hit the wall of the cockpit. *Dong!* "Answer the question, children. Physics. What are the four major forces involved in flight?"

"Gravity?" Evie started to say.

"Shh!" Rick hushed her. "She means weight, 2-Tor. The term is weight. It's the downward force that objects in flight need to fight against to stay in the air."

"Correct, Richard," 2-Tor said. "You have sixty seconds until system shutdown."

The calm and measured way 2-Tor announced that made Evie's stomach curl into knots. "System shutdown? Shutdown?! What's that?"

2-Tor's voice took on a dark, haunting tone. "Your parents linked me to the electrical systems of the *Roost*. I have been instructed not to let you fly anywhere if you do not pass regularly scheduled quizzes. I will disable the *Roost*'s engines if you fail."

Rick's eyes filled with panic. "But we're flying right now, hundreds of feet in the air. You can't shut off the engines—we'll crash."

"You are quite mistaken, Richard." 2-Tor waggled a feather at him. "Sensors show that we are currently parked in front of Lane Mansion."

Evie looked out the window. They had passed Iceland and were over the freezing waters of the Arctic Ocean. If the crash didn't kill them—and it almost certainly would—the freezing waters would do them in.

"Please identify the remaining three major forces of flight."

"This is ridiculous," Rick said. "I'm going to try to land the *Roost* before 2-Tor brings it down."

"That answer is incorrect," 2-Tor said. "Forty-five seconds until system shutdown."

"Can't you just answer the question?" Evie asked.

Rick ignored her, which only served to make Evie even more afraid than she was already. Her brother was always eager to give the answer. Was it possible . . . *he didn't know it?*

Rick pulled on the throttle, but nothing happened. "2-Tor!" he shouted at the robot. "Why can't I pilot the *Roost*?"

2-Tor answered plainly, "It would be dangerous to attempt to administer a quiz while you were distracted by flying the *Roost*. I have initiated the autopilot for your safety."

"This is so messed up!" Evie screamed. "2-Tor, stop this at once."

"That answer is incorrect," 2-Tor said. "Thirty seconds until system shutdown."

"Rick, do something!"

"I'm sorry, Evie. I don't remember. I know I read about it, but I didn't have time to study my physics notes before we left."

Evie took him by the shoulders. "Rick—you have to remember. Please, think!"

"Twenty seconds until system shutdown," 2-Tor said.

"Okay, okay." Rick squeezed his chin like it was about to fall off. "So weight is what pushes the airplane down. In order to prevent that from happening, you need to be able to keep air moving across the wing. This causes . . . um . . . uh . . . lift?"

"Correct. Fifteen seconds remaining."

Rick swallowed hard and took a deep, nervous breath.

"It's okay, Rick," Evie said. "You can do it. I believe in you."

"There's also the force that, um . . . Evie, I can't remember!"

"You can! Think!"

"There's the force that propels the airplane forward. It's called, um, thrust?"

"Correct. Ten seconds remaining. Preparing to disable engines in ten seconds."

"Evie! I can't come up with the last force," Rick said.

"Five seconds remaining."

"Oh no!" Evie wailed. "Having a robot tutor is such a drag."

"Four."

"That's it!" Rick cheered. "Drag! The friction moving between the object and the air. It's air resistance. That's the fourth major force of flight."

"Three."

"What?!" Rick and Evie screamed together.

"Two."

Rick grabbed 2-Tor around the middle and shook him as hard as he could. "2-Tor! Stop the countdown! I got the question right."

"One."

Evie hung on to the back of the pilot's chair. The hum of the hover engines died. Her stomach did a somersault into her throat as the *Roost* plummeted toward the ocean below.

17

ALARMS SCREAMED IN RICK'S EARS. THE *ROOST* FELL LIKE A FLAMING ARROW, FILLING RICK WITH an intense feeling of weightlessness that nearly made him puke. 2-Tor flapped his wings and screeched a sound like a radio blasting Top 40 singles at full volume.

"Rick!" Evie screamed, clinging to him. "We have to do something! Override the system."

"I know!" Rick shouted over the noise.

"Quiz failure! Quiz failure!" 2-Tor squawked.

Rick dove under the flight console and snapped open the access hatch. A mess of colored wires greeted him. "Evie, grab the flight stick. When I reroute the auxiliary power, you're going to have to straighten out the *Roost* so we don't crash."

"I'm already doing it," she said, pulling on the flight stick as hard as she could.

Rick tried to remember how to rewire the ship, but all he could recall was something about an empty socket.

"Impact in ten seconds," 2-Tor screeched.

Rick had had just about enough of countdowns.

And then he saw it, a vacant white socket behind the wires, looking at him like a surprised ghost. He disconnected the main power plug and stuck it into the auxiliary socket.

A million needles struck his arm all at once. He recoiled in pain at the electric shock. "Argh!"

2-Tor's voice sounded distant and tired. "Power restored. System operational."

The reactivation of the *Roost*'s engines screeched like a robot symphony.

"Woo-hoo!" Evie cheered, pulling back on the flight stick. But then she said the worst two syllables Rick had ever heard her say. "Uh-oh."

"'Uh-oh'? What's uh-oh?" Rick asked, climbing out from under the dashboard.

The flight stick shook violently, and Evie struggled to keep her grip on it. "Umm . . . we're coming in a little bit too fast."

"A little? We're going two hundred miles per hour! Pull up, Evie! Pull up!"

He put his hands over hers and pulled with all his might. Together they adjusted the angle of the *Roost* so that the engines pushed down, allowing the repulsor buffer to kick in.

But still they fell.

Rick held his breath as the bright blue ocean filled the windshield.

Then everything went black as the *Roost* hit the surface, cutting through the dark water like a diving rod. Rick toppled to the cockpit floor. 2-Tor lost his balance and tipped over. Rick rolled out of the way just an instant before 2-Tor struck the floor with a tremendous *DONG* that echoed throughout the hovership.

Being wood, the *Roost* floated, bobbing to the surface a few seconds later. The hovership balanced on the ocean like a message in a bottle, upright with quite a bit of tilting.

Evie crawled out from under the control console. She put a hand over her chest, gasping for breath. "We made it."

Rick flipped 2-Tor over and inspected the front of his robot body. "2-Tor, are you okay?"

2-Tor's eyes shot sparks. "Internal battery functioning at nine percent."

"What got into you, you stupid bird?" Rick asked.

2-Tor tapped his feathers together awkwardly. "When I was exposed to the electromagnetic pulse from your father's detention device, it must have corrupted some of my memory. My solid-state drive contains all the programs and code, millions and millions of lines, that allow me to function. Some subsection of my master program must have been altered, or damaged, creating the series of catastrophic errors we just experienced. By my bolts, I am so embarrassed. I am sorry, children. Are you all right?"

"We're fine," Rick said, unable to help but smile at the silly robot. "We're just glad you're okay."

"If there is anything I can do to make it up to you, I will. Both of you will receive extra scoops of ice cream every dessert for a week."

"How about for a year?" Evie fanned herself with her hand for effect. "I'm a little traumatized over here."

"I will make it a month," 2-Tor said. "But do not push it, young lady."

Rick rose to his feet and helped 2-Tor up. "As much as I love ice cream, we need to figure out what to do next."

"Isn't it obvious?" Evie replied. "Look at our GPS. We're only about fifty miles from the coordinates you found at Winterpole HQ. We should fly there right away."

Rick took a glance for himself, then agreed. "You're right. We should go find the seastead, but how about we stay in the water? I've had enough air travel for a while."

"It's a deal," Evie said, pushing the lever to increase the throttle. The hover engines spat bubbles, and the *Roost* cut through the water like a snorkel.

Besides the low rumble of the engines, the trip was peaceful. It felt good to have some quiet after the intense landing. 2-Tor kept to himself, standing half in and half out of the cockpit, almost as if he was ashamed to be in the same room as Rick and Evie. Rick felt bad. He didn't want a depressed robot on this trip. It wasn't even 2-Tor's fault. Like everything else, the problems went back to Winterpole.

Evie distracted him from his brooding. "The coordinates are pretty close to the North Pole."

"I guess they are," Rick agreed, sitting forward in the pilot's chair.

"Do you think Doctor Grant lives at the North Pole?"

"I don't think so."

"What if Doctor Grant is Santa Claus?"

"Don't be ridiculous."

"What if he *is*, though?"

"He's not."

"I'm not saying he is. I'm saying *what* if he is."

"Evie! Dad's old teacher is *not* Santa Claus."

His sister rolled her eyes. "Sheesh. What a grinch."

They drove into a chain of icebergs, which dotted the water like the little bars of soap Mom used to throw into Rick's baths. He knew from his reading that some icebergs were more than a hundred meters tall, although most of their mass was hidden under the water.

"Look at that!" Evie said, pointing at two large blobs on the GPS. "There are whales swimming alongside the *Roost*. AWWOOOOOOOOOH!"

"What's that?" Rick asked. "Your whale call?"

Evie ignored the jab. "I sing to thee, gentle giants of the ocean. AWWOOOOOOOOOH!!!!!"

"You sound like a wolf."

"AWWOOOOOOOOOH!!!" She howled in his face. "It's a whale. Rick, you better clean the blubber out of your ears. That sounds nothing like a wolf."

"Children . . ." There were long pauses between 2-Tor's quiet words. "My sensors indicate that we are directly on top of the coordinates of Doctor Grant's seastead. I'm not sure if you can trust my sensors after the terrible thing that I did, but that is what they say."

"It's all right, 2-Tor," Rick assured the robot. "The GPS says the same thing."

"So where is it?" Evie asked, peering out the windows. "What are we looking for?"

When Rick closed his eyes, he could see Doctor Grant's incredible invention. A seastead—an artificial island capable of housing hundreds if not thousands of people. It would look a little like an oil rig, but much bigger, and more beautiful. From above, it would resemble the most tranquil homestead imaginable. Happy families would toss Frisbees and walk their dogs. Teachers would hold classes in outdoor gazebos, where kids could run and play between lessons. Maybe there would even be an aviary to house all the birds that wanted to visit. It would be heaven—a perfect place where Rick could read books and play video games and no one would bother him, where he could continue the mission of Lane Industries to develop cutting-edge technologies.

"No sign of anything anywhere," Evie said for the eightieth time. Doctor Grant's seastead would only be heaven if they could find it. . . .

"I don't understand." Rick furrowed his brow. "We detected those whales on the GPS, and there are icebergs everywhere. Why hasn't the seastead appeared on our scanners?"

"I'm checking them." Evie adjusted the dials, focusing the three-dimensional map the *Roost* had charted of the area. "But I don't see anything."

Rick moved his eyes close to the GPS screen, peering over the graphics for any hint of the seastead's location.

The giant structure should have been easy to spot.

For over an hour they drifted in circles, looking behind icebergs in search of Doctor Grant's elusive ocean hideout. Rick was tired, Evie was bored, and they both really could have gone for a chicken sandwich.

"It's no use!" Evie banged her fist on the console. "There's nothing up here."

"Wait a minute!" Rick grabbed the GPS screen and pulled his face closer to it. "Straight ahead. What's that?"

Evie peered out the windshield. "I don't know. It's bright. Something reflective."

"Is it some kind of hovercraft?" Rick asked.

"I can't be sure from here," Evie said. "Let's get a closer look."

"Wait! It might be dangerous," Rick cautioned.

"Only one way to find out!" Evie grinned, pushing the *Roost* forward.

Ahead in the windshield, Rick watched as the bright reflective light took shape. It was a flat raft of what looked like plastic bottles, bound together with hundreds of tight rubber bands.

"Come on!" Evie said, jumping out of her seat. "Let's go check it out."

Rick raced her through the *Roost*. They emerged from a knot large enough for them to stand in and crept onto one of the longer branches overlooking the plastic bottle raft. There was a bunch of junk at the bottom of the raft—cooking gear, a small stove, a broken radio, a big bundle of rags, and a small pile of fish bones.

Asleep on the edge of the raft was a long, thin cat with reddish-brown fur and black stripes. It looked a little bit like a tiger.

"It's just a cat," Evie said.

"*Rrrrowa!*" said the tiger cat.

The pile of rags shook. "Quiet, Niels Bohr! Quiet, I say!"

The tiger cat hissed, then padded in a circle around the bobbing raft. Rick watched in disbelief as the pile of rags fell apart, revealing an old man in huge bug-eyed sunglasses.

"Excuse me, sir!" Rick called out to him. He waved, but the man seemed uninterested in the two children on the seafaring tree. "I'm looking for a seastead that's supposed to be around here. It should look a little bit like an oil rig, but with houses and stuff on it. Have you seen anything like that?"

The old man snorted. "Seen? Nope! I haven't seen anything. You see, I'm blind! But as for the seastead, you're looking at it. Welcome! You've arrived!"

2-Tor pushed his way through the knot and sidled onto the branch. He dug his talons into the wood to keep from falling off. "I say! What's going on here?"

Rick could not understand what the old blind man was talking about. How could this ugly recycled raft be the seastead? The seastead was supposed to be a palace on the waves, a worthy home for someone of Doctor Grant's genius.

He called out to the old man, "I don't understand. Where's Doctor Grant?"

"You're looking at him!" the old blind man said.

"Assuming you're not blind too. And if I could see, I would be looking at Richard and Evelyn Lane."

Rick exchanged a glance with Evie, who appeared equally surprised. "I'm not sure which is more confusing," she began in what for her was a tentative tone, "that you are Doctor Grant, or that you know who we are."

Doctor Grant cackled. "You mean I was right? Stupendous!"

Evie squinted like she was trying to read fine print. "Did our dad tell you we were coming?"

"No, I have not spoken to your father in well over a decade, but I would recognize the sound of a robo-voci speech box anywhere. Only George Lane could fine-tune such a brilliant invention."

2-Tor sounded startled. "You mean me, sir?"

"Yes, yes!" Doctor Grant said, moving his head around as if trying to find where 2-Tor was standing above him. "You sound like a marvelous creation."

"Why, sir, my coils are blushing. No one has ever said that about me before."

Doctor Grant slapped his knee and laughed. "This is too much. So where is the old circuit dealer?"

"You mean our dad?" Evie asked. "He's in trouble. That's why we came. Doctor Grant, we need your help."

The blind doctor called them down from the *Roost*. The water was too unstable to use the ship's exit ramp, so Rick fetched a grappling hook. 2-Tor stayed on the branch overlooking the raft, while Rick and Evie climbed down the grappling hook's rope and settled on Doctor

Grant's water bottle abode. It was no larger than a king-sized bed.

"I still don't understand how this can be the seastead," Rick said. "I expected something so much bigger."

Doctor Grant scowled. "So did I! But then Winterpole and Mastercorp and a hundred other pests started sticking their noses into my business. I couldn't have them spotting my hideout from a reconnaissance hovership, could I? For now, this is the best I can do. So I continue my experiments in private. Away from Winterpole. Away from Mastercorp. I like it. It's peaceful. Just me and Niels Bohr."

"Niels Bohr?" Rick asked. "The Danish physicist? But he's been dead for decades."

"No! How can that be? Niels Bohr! Where are you?" Doctor Grant started to cry. "I just fed him an hour ago. The most delicious char. Poor Niels Bohr."

"*Mrrrowl!*" said the tiger cat, pouncing into Doctor Grant's lap.

The doctor clutched the cat gratefully. "Oh, Niels Bohr! There you are. Thank goodness you're alive. I thought I'd lost you forever, you silly kitty."

Evie couldn't stop laughing. Her face turned purple. "Hahaha heehoohoo. Ha ha. Rick, you're such a doof. He named the cat Niels Bohr. Ha ha ha. I can't breathe."

Rick scowled. "Laugh it up, Evie. Go on. Get it out."

"You told him his cat was dead. He was so upset. Ha ha ha ha ha."

Rick looked at Doctor Grant, who was giving Niels Bohr

Eskimo kisses. "I'm sorry I told you your cat was dead, Doctor Grant. I was confused."

"It's all right," Doctor Grant said while the cat licked his face. "As long as my tiger is all right."

"Why did you name the cat Niels Bohr, anyway?"

"Kitty litter. That's all I'll say. So, children, what has brought you all the way out here? And how can this old wayward scientist be of service to you?"

Evie and Rick told him everything—about their trip to see the garbage patch, about what Winterpole had done to their father and how they'd tried to free him, about their escape from Winterpole Headquarters, and all the way up to their death-defying trip across the ocean to find the seastead.

When they finished their tale, Doctor Grant sat back and scratched his chin as their father often did. After a ponderous silence, he said, "I think I see, no pun intended. Winterpole is persecuting your father. He needs a safe haven. You want to terraform the Great Pacific Garbage Patch into an eighth continent. There, Winterpole will have no jurisdiction. You will be free. I have just one question. What does any of this have to do with me?"

Rick pulled his portable hard drive out of his pocket. "You can't see it, but I'm holding a special item in my hand. It's my father's half of the Eden Compound. We need your half to complete the formula."

"Oh!" Doctor Grant said. "Well, why didn't you say so? I could have saved us all a lot of time and trouble. The answer is no. I will not give you my half of the formula."

18

EVIE THOUGHT THAT SHE MIGHT NEED A Q-TIP THE SIZE OF A CANOE OAR TO CLEAN OUT HER EARS.

Had she heard the old scientist correctly? Had he really just said that he wouldn't help them?

"Doctor Grant, using the Eden Compound is really important to my family. Dad needs a safe place to do his experiments. We need to get away from our rotten classmates."

"Those are selfish reasons. Your father doesn't need a new lab. He needs to stop stealing birds from wilderness preserves."

His words burned deep. That label was unfair. Her father had been trying to save that bird, not steal it. Now he would be labeled as a criminal forever, and it was all Winterpole's fault.

Pushing the thought from her mind, Evie leaned forward. "You could live with us on the eighth continent. It will be warm and peaceful. There will be lots of space where Niels Bohr can play. You will have your own lab, where you can work on building a real seastead, or any experiment you wish."

"That sounds lovely," Doctor Grant said.

Hope filled Evie's chest like fluffy clouds. "Doesn't it?"

"Yes. I'm eager to see how you make your continent without the Eden Compound."

"But that's impossible!"

"Not my problem!" Doctor Grant hissed. "Did you ever think to ask why I am so opposed to this? The Eden Compound doesn't just transform garbage. It converts all forms of inorganic matter. You want to know why Mastercorp funded our project? You think it was because of their concern for the environment? They wanted to use it as a weapon. Imagine if the Eden Compound was sprayed over a city. Every building destroyed. Millions killed. Mass hysteria. In the wrong hands, the Eden Compound could send humankind back to the Stone Age!"

Annoyance crept into Evie's voice. "We've heard all this before, Doctor Grant."

"Then you should know my answer!"

Evie saw her future slipping away. She needed Doctor Grant. Without him there would be no Eden Compound and no eighth continent. She understood what he was trying to say. The risks involved in using the Eden Compound were high. For years Doctor Grant had protected the secrets of the formula from Mastercorp and Winterpole, but there were so many reasons to make a new continent free from outside intrusion. She didn't want it just for her family, but for everyone in the world.

When Evie next spoke, she was surprised by the quaver in her voice. "Doctor Grant, don't you see? The power of the Eden Compound is the reason we have to be the ones to use it. You and my father invented it so that you could get rid of all the trash that is choking this planet. Your intentions were noble. We want to continue your mission now. Have you seen the Great Pacific Garbage Patch, Doctor Grant? It's bigger than any living organism, a swirling mass of plastic bags and bottles and filth. The fish die. The birds starve. The patch is killing huge communities of plankton—you know, the little sea creatures that make the ecosystem work. We want to destroy that mess, Doctor, and replace it with a continent of nature and beauty, something that the entire world can enjoy. We don't want the Eden Compound to fall into the wrong hands any more than you do. If you help us make the eighth continent, when we're done we can erase the formula together, so that it can never be used as a weapon, like you fear it will be. Please, Doctor Grant. Help us. Help us save the world."

The old doctor listened to her speech in silence, nodding occasionally and stroking Niels Bohr under his chin. At last Evie finished, breathlessly, and sat down on the raft. She shivered in the freezing air.

Doctor Grant slapped his thighs, startling Niels Bohr. "Well, when you put it that way, my dear. All right. I'm in." He snapped at Rick. "Pay attention to your sister, my boy. She is very intelligent. You could learn a thing or six from her."

The look on Rick's face was worth all the trouble they had been through to get here.

"Sweet!" Evie cheered in relief. "So, what do we do next? Where is your half of the formula?"

"The formula?" Doctor Grant repeated. "Oh, right. I forgot. I don't have it!"

"What?!" Evie buried her face in her hands. After all this, they still didn't have the Eden Compound.

"However," the doctor said, "I know where it is."

"That's great," Rick said. "Which way do we need to go?"

Doctor Grant showed his crooked teeth in a big grin. He pointed straight down at the ocean.

19

IN THE DEEP DARKNESS OF THE SEA, RICK TRIED NOT TO PANIC. HE SWAM CLOSE BEHIND EVIE AND Doctor Grant, watching their flippers alternate up and down. He hoped it wouldn't be much farther. His legs were starting to cramp.

Although the *Roost*'s storage hold contained scuba gear in twelve sizes, he'd never tried any of the equipment on. He knew that *scuba* was an acronym for "self-contained underwater breathing apparatus," but that's about all that he knew about the device. Being underwater, with fish swimming past his head and the pressure of the ocean pushing against his ribs, it took time for him to remember to breathe. His innate reaction was to hold his breath, and so until he ran out of air he would hold it, even though his respirator was snug in his mouth. With each wheezy gasp, he made a mental note to try to breathe normally, but the strange surroundings and the fear of drowning kept making him forget.

In most of the video games Rick played, the depths of

the ocean were home to killer sharks, giant squids, electric eels, flesh-eating piranhas, poisonous jellyfish, and starfish. (Obviously starfish did not sound as dangerous as the other creatures on his list, but he refused to trust anything that had no head.) Rick feared all of these sea monsters. He had seen no evidence that a wetsuit and scuba tank would keep him safe, but he had plenty of evidence that staying on dry land would.

When Rick had expressed his reservations about swimming underwater, Doctor Grant's response was unsympathetic, at best. "If a seventy-year-old blind scientist with a bum hip and bad teeth can swim two miles underwater, then so can you!"

Yeah, Rick thought, watching the old man paddle in front of him, *but Doctor Grant has an aquatic echo locator device to help him find his way in the dark ocean.* All Rick had were the sniffles.

Still, he tried his best, staying close so that he wouldn't get lost. They could only see a few meters ahead in the dark water. If he swam too far to one side, or fell too far behind, Evie and Doctor Grant would disappear, and Rick would be lost alone in the gut of the ocean.

Scuba diving was the *worst*. Rick was used to swimming by repeatedly mashing the *X*-button, not by kicking his legs.

Evie had taken to the water like a duck to, well, water. Her flippers moved in a blur, and frequently she had to slow down so that Rick and Doctor Grant could catch up. Rick wanted to scold her for racing ahead, but with the respirator in his mouth, he couldn't complain.

Part of Rick's trouble catching up came from his constantly having to stop to drain his face mask. His glasses left little gaps in the plastic seal around his face, which meant the little pouch for his nose was constantly filling up with water.

Just when Rick thought he was going to be swimming forever, he saw it, a black shadow emerging from the darkness. At first he thought it was a whale, although the massive thing suspended in the water was bigger than any whale Rick knew about. Its fins were outstretched, and a heavy propeller was embedded in each. As they got closer, Rick realized that he wasn't looking at a whale but at a submarine, the largest he had ever seen, bigger than the entire campus of ISES.

He recalled Doctor Grant's words while they were suiting up. "After your father and I parted ways, Mastercorp was not pleased with the lack of results our project—and their money—had produced. I owed them, they said. I was taken to a giant submarine research facility under the Arctic Ocean, where I was forced to conduct tests, create weapons, and attempt to generate the Eden Compound. They held me in solitary confinement. They denied me food. But still I would not re-create the formula. They found my half. It was confiscated when they raided my lab. They tried to replicate the compound themselves, but without the half your father had, they failed. Eventually I sabotaged the facility and escaped. During my travels, hiding around the world, I returned to the lab several times. It's been abandoned for years, but it still had working equipment that I could salvage. Now we can use it to fabricate the Eden Compound."

They swam up to the hull of the submarine and paddled alongside it. Painted on the side of the hull were the words MSS *Cichlid*. Clever, Rick thought. African cichlids were some of the most intelligent fish in the world. A perfect name for an underwater science facility.

Feeling the exterior of the massive vessel with his hands, Doctor Grant found his bearings and led them to an access hatch. He punched a few numbers into a keypad on the hatch, and the door irised open.

Startled, Rick felt a strange pulling sensation.

He tried to swim away, but water spiraled into the open hatch like it was rushing down the drain of a sink. Doctor Grant flew in immediately, and then Evie was swallowed.

Rick fought against the current until his arms gave out. He banged his elbow against the hatch as he fell inside, sending sparks of pain through his arm.

Wherever he was, it was cold and flooded. He couldn't see an inch in front of his face. He groped wildly for something to grab onto, realizing that in this dark place blind Doctor Grant wasn't really at a disadvantage.

His hands settled on the sleek fabric of Evie's wetsuit. It didn't matter if she teased him for hugging her—he was scared.

He heard a loud gurgling sound, like the pipes of an old house. The water was draining out of this chamber, which must have been some kind of airlock—a way for people to enter and exit the research sub without flooding the whole vessel.

Rick sniffed and almost gagged. Even with their masks on, Evie's breath *stank* of fish. He knew she shouldn't have eaten that leftover char.

When the water had all gurgled away, red emergency lights came on. Evie and Doctor Grant were standing together at the far end of the small chamber, pulling off their masks and mouthpieces, gulping the stale air.

Wait. Evie? Then who was Rick—

It wasn't clear who was more surprised, Rick or the gray seal he was hugging. They both howled in alarm and pulled away.

Evie cackled madly. "Rick! I didn't know you had a *girl*friend."

"*Raaaawf!*" said the seal, not amused.

"That seal must have gotten pulled into the airlock with us when we entered the sub. No worries. We will let him out when we're finished here." Doctor Grant unzipped his satchel and pulled out a glass container the size of a lunchbox, a respirator attached to the side. He popped it open with a hiss.

An agitated Niels Bohr was curled up inside. The tiger cat leaped out of the box, looking as unhappy to be there as the seal.

"I'm sorry, Niels Bohr. They didn't have any scuba gear in your size."

"Mrowl! Rowl!" Niels Bohr mewed, annoyed.

Rick took stock of their surroundings. They were in a small room with three doors leading off in different directions. To him the doors all looked the same. "So which way do we go?" he asked.

"This way," Doctor Grant said, opening one of the doors, which revealed a long, rusty hallway beyond.

The seal barked as they left. He did not seem to appreciate being left alone.

20

AT LEAST THE HALLWAY HAD BETTER LIGHTING, EVIE THOUGHT AS THEY PASSED BY SEVERAL laboratories. Most of the windows looking into the labs were shattered. Shards of glass stuck out from the window frames like the maws of sharks.

The inside of the labs were just as run down. Tarps covered most of the equipment. Any exposed devices and computer terminals appeared to be broken.

"What's down here?" Evie asked, opening a door.

In the next room they saw a number of chambers, sectioned off into glass enclosures. Long tubes of bottled electricity ran along the ceiling. The occasional flash filled the room with multicolored light.

Evie's eyes widened in amazement. "Wow, what's this?!"

Rick adjusted his glasses. "It's a thermal-charge power plant. Fascinating."

Doctor Grant laughed. "My dear boy! How did you know that?"

139

"One second," Rick said, his eyes darting from chamber to chamber. "I want to see a release."

They watched in silence for a moment. A valve opened at the top of one of the chambers. In an instant, the chamber was flooded with bright orange heat. They recoiled as a wave of hot air passed over them.

"Yow!" Evie rubbed her arm, which was a little pink. "I'm scorched!"

"I can't believe it!" Rick slicked back his damp hair with his hands. "A working thermal-charge power plant, in the middle of the ocean! I didn't think these existed in real life."

"This one does," Doctor Grant said. "I should know. I built it."

"How does it work?" Evie asked, continuing to be amazed by the old doctor.

"Just like a volcano," Rick explained, grinning like a mad scientist. "You have molten rock and apply pressure to it. The rock superheats, forcing it through a channel at tremendous velocity, generating more energy than you applied."

"So you're creating little volcanic eruptions on a submarine." Evie nodded sarcastically. "Sounds safe."

Rick pressed his hand against the wall of the submarine, feeling the thrum of scientific progress. "The magma generated by the process has to go somewhere. That's these release chambers."

"Correct," Doctor Grant said. "It worked better than I'd ever hoped. My volcano engine has been powering the

Cichlid for years without any maintenance."

"Can we go inside and take a closer look?" Rick asked, sounding giddier than Evie on a mission with Dad.

"Are you crazy?" Doctor Grant gave him a pat on top of the head. "Don't you know how dangerous it is in there? If you somehow got trapped in one of those release chambers, the blast of thermal energy would vaporize you! Do you know what that means? Not even your bones would be left behind!"

"But you just said it has never needed maintenance."

"I know! Isn't that nuts? It could break any second. Now, follow me. Do you want an eighth continent or don't you? We're wasting time."

Doctor Grant led Rick and Evie through the narrow corridors, while Niels Bohr purred and followed. When they reached a large lab at the end of a hallway, the doctor steered them inside.

This lab looked different from the others. While most of the *Cichlid* was in damaged disarray, this room was pristine. Everything was in its place. The chairs were upright. The tables were pushed against the walls. The tarps were neatly folded in a stack in one corner. Everything was dusted.

"Ah, back at last," Doctor Grant said. "Even the floor feels right." He walked with confidence to the far side of the room, where he booted up a computer terminal. The bright overhead fluorescent lights came on, hurting Rick's eyes after so much time in darkness and dimness.

At first Evie was confused that Doctor Grant was staring

intently at the illuminated computer monitor in front of him, but then she saw that next to his keyboard was a kind of computer tablet she had never seen before. The screen was made of an almost jelly-like material that rippled whenever Doctor Grant typed something or switched screens. It was some kind of smart Braille tablet that changed its arrangement of dots so the doctor could read with just his fingers. It was clear where Evie's father had gotten so much of his inspiration.

He pointed to a computer terminal on the far side of the room. "Rick, I want you to upload your father's half of the formula to that data bay. Evie, be a dear and bring me the bag of reagents from that fridge over there."

"Reagents?" Evie asked.

"It means *ingredients*," Rick explained.

"I know what reagents are," Evie called over her shoulder as she walked to the fridge. "What are you, a boy alchemist?"

"Enough!" Doctor Grant said, irritation creeping into his voice. "I'm violating a solemn oath I made to myself to help you create this eighth continent of yours. I won't have you bickering while I do it."

Rick plugged his thumb drive into the big data bay and uploaded the file. Evie lugged the bag of reagents to Doctor Grant's desk. "Hoo boy!" Evie said, fanning her nose. "That fridge smells awful! There's a can of tuna in there that I think is left over from the late Devonian period."

At the word *tuna*, Niels Bohr attacked the refrigerator

with a vengeance. The humans ignored him.

Both halves of the Eden Compound formula appeared on Doctor Grant's screen. He snorted with glee. "George, you whippersnapper. Look at this. Your father managed to update the formula with just his half. He has done quite a bit of work."

"What does that mean?" Rick asked.

"Two things. One, your father is a genius, but we already knew that. Two, it means this process will be much quicker than I initially anticipated."

Rick leaned over Doctor Grant's shoulder and squinted at the monitor. "How long will it take you to update your half of the formula and create a prototype batch of the compound?"

"Not long at all," Doctor Grant said. "Twelve to eighteen hours."

"What?! That's almost a whole day. We don't have time for that."

Evie looked around the dank lab nervously. "You mean . . . we are going to have to sleep here?"

"I'm afraid so. I'll work through the night to get it done. You kids should try to take a snooze, and I'll wake you when I'm finished."

Rick's stomach grumbled. "What about dinner?"

Doctor Grant said, "Hmm . . . better hurry. Niels Bohr is going to eat all the tuna."

21

RICK AND EVIE FOUND AN EMPTY STORAGE CLOSET OFF DOCTOR GRANT'S LAB WHERE THEY COULD bed down for a few hours of rest. They used some tarps for blankets and bunched up others for pillows.

With Niels Bohr's leftovers in their bellies and the echoey sound of water dripping as a lullaby, they drifted into a restful state.

Rick was not sure how long he had been asleep when his sister's words woke him.

"Rick?"

". . ."

"Rick?"

". . ."

"Hey, Rick!"

". . . What?"

"Are you awake?"

"I am now, Evie."

The plastic tarps crinkled as she rolled onto her side. Even in the darkness he could see the hopeful look on her face.

"Do you think the Eden Compound will really work as well as they said?"

"I don't know. You dragged 2-Tor and me around the world, so I hope *you* have confidence."

"I think it will work. I just wanted to see if you did."

"Since when did my opinion mean anything to you?"

She was quiet for a while.

"It always has. I just don't tell you about it."

"How come?"

"Are you kidding? Because you'd lord it over me like some . . . lord!"

"Wow. Evie Lane. Hanging on the word of her big brother."

She nudged him playfully. "See! This is why I didn't want to tell you!"

They shared a smile and went silent again.

"Rick?"

"Yeah?"

"Do you . . . do you want to build the eighth continent?"

"What do you mean?"

"I think our whole adventure is kind of fun, but you always seem so miserable."

"Risking our lives is not exactly my idea of fun."

"Please tell me. Do you want to build the continent?"

He stared up at the ceiling, twisted with pipes. "I thought I did. Building a whole new world from scratch? Sounds like a supercool video game, in real life! But the more I think how we are doing it to help Dad, I get angry. We shouldn't have to help Dad. He's Dad! He should be looking out for us! Instead, he's always making a bungle of things. He's the reason we're in this mess."

"Dad is brilliant, though."

"Sometimes I think there are two dads. There's Brilliant Dad, and there's Wacky Dad. Brilliant Dad built the *Roost*. Wacky Dad wants to punch a garbage dump's lights out. You like Wacky Dad. I would be happy if he was just Brilliant Dad."

"He's our family. You have to trust that he is always brilliant."

"But he *did* break Winterpole's rules."

"Rick, I would do everything I could to help you, even if you stole a million Popsicles."

"Even if I stole a million and one Popsicles?"

Evie yawned loudly, smiling. "Even if you stole a million and one Popsicles."

"I don't know if the Eden Compound will work, but I hope it does. For you. Because we're family."

". . ."

"Evie?"

But his baby sister was fast asleep, Niels Bohr snuggled underneath her chin.

Rick lay in the darkness for a long time, his thoughts twisting like the pipes on the ceiling. Images in his mind of his father and the garbage patch kept him awake. This was frustrating. Without enough sleep, he would never recharge his energy bar.

If he wasn't going to sleep, he figured he might as well learn something. He slipped out from under the canvas covers and went exploring.

When he opened the closet door, the lab was dark, but Doctor Grant was still awake, typing furiously on the keyboard at his computer terminal. He stopped abruptly when Rick entered the room.

"Richard. A word."

Timidly, Rick approached.

"Have you ever asked your father why he is on a mission to rid the world of trash?"

"I assume it's because he recognizes that garbage is pollution. Pollution is bad for the environment. No surprise there."

"Lots of people recognize that, Richard. Why do you think your dad is so impassioned about this issue that he's made it his lifelong purpose?"

"Um . . . I, uh, don't know." Rick was surprised hearing himself say the words. Could it be true that in all this time he had never asked his father about the origins of his prime obsession?

"You don't seem to have much confidence in him."

"Well, the stuff he does doesn't make sense half the time."

Doctor Grant inhaled deeply, almost as if he was meditating. "Your sister trusts him on blind faith. She doesn't need an explanation."

"She doesn't make sense half the time, either."

"Your father was born in trash, you know."

"What do you mean?" He couldn't process what he was hearing. "My father grew up the son of Jonas Lane, the billionaire founder of Lane Industries."

Doctor Grant's next words were like a chasm opening under Rick's feet. "He grew up the son of Jonas Lane, but he was not born that way. He was found in a black garbage bag by the caretaker of a dump. The caretaker took him in, but the man and his wife were wicked, and as soon as George was old enough to walk, they put him to work. For five years he served the caretaker, until by chance a woman walking past saw a little boy shoveling filth in the hot sun. She phoned social services, which took your father away. Over a year he lived in an orphanage, until Jonas Lane and his wife came looking to adopt a little boy. Jonas saw at once there was a spark of creativity in little George. One day he would make a fitting heir. From that point onward, your father had a happy childhood. When he was my student, he often regaled me with stories of the bird-watching trips his father took him on as a boy. He loved to watch birds fly, Rick. He loved the freedom they had—freedom he lacked when he was living in the garbage dump."

Rick realized that twice in the past year his father had offered to take him bird-watching, but the first time he had needed to study for a test, and the second he had been competing in a video game tournament at the mall. Suddenly, he felt like more of a monster than that caretaker.

"The birds were what inspired your father to invent the hover engine. He wanted to fly. And my, how he has flown.

He researched terraforming with me because he had seen children all over the world living in filth, in squalor. No one deserved what he had suffered, he thought, and so he found his purpose."

Still trying to grapple with what Doctor Grant was saying, Rick stuttered, "So, we're not really Lanes?"

Doctor Grant reached out, grabbing Rick by either side of the head, and pulled him close. "You are your father's son. Do not forget it. I may be blind, but I see it in your intelligence, in your curiosity, in your stubbornness."

"Me?! Evie is the stubborn one."

"Listen to yourself. See? Stubborn."

Rick pulled away and ran out of the lab as fast as he could. He gasped for breath, each footfall a deafening echo in the hollow submarine.

How could his parents have never told him any of this? He was eleven years old. He deserved to know the truth. Dad was adopted. All Rick had ever wanted was to guide the future of Lane Industries, and he wasn't even a Lane. Meanwhile, he always accused his father of not having purpose, when the opposite was true. Now Rick was the one who was confused, without any direction, and his father, with all his noble goals, was the one to follow and admire.

"I've been so stupid!" Rick wept as he ran through the *Cichlid*. It was the hardest thing he'd ever admitted to himself.

When he ran out of breath, Rick collapsed on the floor. Eventually he pulled himself to his feet and realized that he was totally lost. He began to retrace his steps, hoping to find his way back to Doctor Grant and his sister.

The other laboratories were in such disrepair that it was hard to tell what kind of work they'd been doing there. There was a lab where big craters had been smashed into the metal floor, and broken machinery lay scattered everywhere.

Another lab contained an empty weapons rack and plastic things that shouldn't have been plastic. Fruit, teddy bears, guacamole. Target practice? Some kind of plastic-making gun?

Twice Rick passed by a door without noticing it, until finally the black painted door on the black wall caught his eye. To most, the concealed door, the heavy lock (which had long fallen off), and the general spookiness of the secret lab would have meant "Keep Out," but to Rick it meant "Hidden Area. Sweet."

Sometimes his desire to explore 100 percent of the map overpowered even his fear of the unknown.

Rick opened the black door.

What he saw inside the room made the tuna in his stomach creep up his throat and try to escape out of his mouth. White broken bones lay scattered on the floor. The skulls of bulls and tigers and hammerhead sharks were among the morbid clutter, along with dozens of cracked rib cages and leg bones, like the remains of a discarded chicken dinner.

Everything in Rick's mind was telling him to run—to get away from there as fast as possible—but he held his ground. The only way not to fear this place was to know it.

Littered among the bones were the battered exo-hulls of old robots. An arm here, a torso there. It almost looked like the animal bones and the robot bodies . . . belonged together.

On a table, a stack of damp papers had spread and soaked, leaving a thick patina of gray mush. On the top sheet, Rick could make out a single word.

ANIARMAMENT.

A cold hand clamped down on Rick's shoulder. This proved to be a bit too much unknowingness. Rick screamed like his server was down for maintenance.

"Rick!" a startled Doctor Grant exclaimed, squeezing him a little tighter. "You scared me."

"Look who's talking!" Rick gasped.

"I've been trying to find you. I was worried."

"I got lost," he admitted. "What is this place?"

"I don't know," Doctor Grant said stiffly. "They never let me in here."

"I wonder what these experiments were for. What was Mastercorp up to?"

"Come on," Doctor Grant said. "We can't worry about that now. The formula is done. It's time to test the Eden Compound."

When they returned to Doctor Grant's lab, Evie was awake and standing near the center testing table with Niels Bohr. She rubbed her eyes like she was kneading raw dough.

"I was dreaming about chocolate," she said. "Do we have any chocolate?"

"No," Doctor Grant said plainly. "But we have some Eden Compound. Why don't we try that out?"

"Way better than chocolate!" Evie beamed, the tiredness promptly disappearing from her eyes.

Doctor Grant was obviously unmoved on the subject of chocolate because he continued issuing directions. "Evie, grab that bag of trash over by the door and put it in the dispersal zone. Rick, please join me by the main console."

The kids did as they were ordered. Evie picked up the bag of trash, which was mostly crumpled printer paper and empty tuna fish cans, and placed it on the table in the main testing area. There was a bull's-eye painted on the surface where she set it down, under a dry sprinkler nozzle.

Doctor Grant slumped into his chair in front of the computer terminal, Rick standing beside him. The doctor's fingers tap-danced on the keyboard, booting up a custom computer program. "After reassembling the formula, I fabricated a small test batch of Eden Compound. Just a few milliliters, but it should be enough to terraform this garbage bag into living, organic matter, as our early tests predicted. If this test is successful, we will produce a big batch, and then it's off to the Pacific Ocean to make your continent. Saving the environment before breakfast. That's my kind of work!"

Evie obviously agreed. "I can't wait!" she said. "Let's go!!!!"

Rick could barely believe it. After all the work they had done to get to this moment, to the Eden Compound, it was finally happening. They had found Doctor Grant.

They were really going to make the eighth continent. Rick tried to imagine what it would be like: his own world to run and organize. He would be such a better arbiter than Winterpole ever was. He would create a peaceful, intelligent society, one where people would be free to pursue scientific endeavors and play all the video games they wanted.

And he would make his father proud.

Evie was so excited she was bouncing up and down like one of Dad's self-piloting pogo sticks. Rick was glad to see her smile. He had meant what he'd said to her. He wanted her crazy plan to work, for her. He wanted her to be happy.

Doctor Grant threw the switch, and the pipes thrummed, and the liquefied Eden Compound surged toward the sprinkler. Rick could feel the dream of the eighth continent becoming real.

The sprinkler opened up, and thin green liquid shot out in a cone. It ran over the outside of the garbage bag in sheets, coating it like a candied apple. The cool smell of ozone filled Rick's nose.

He watched carefully, waiting for the trash bag to change.

He kept watching.

The sprinkler dribbled to a stop. The green liquid pooled underneath the bag of garbage. The bag hadn't changed. None of the garbage had.

The Eden Compound didn't work.

22

EVIE BACKED AWAY FROM THE DISPERSAL DEVICE. "WHAT? NO! HOW CAN IT NOT WORK?"

"Evie, calm down!" Rick begged.

She turned on Doctor Grant. "You said it would work! Why won't it work?"

Doctor Grant looked like he had caught a skunk by surprise. "Go stick your head in an igloo and cool it, you spicy potato chip. All I know is that I reassembled the formula and produced a sample of the compound based on our designs."

"I'm sorry." She hung her head. "I didn't mean to shout. It's just that we are so close, and now I don't know what to do. How can it not work?"

Evie felt like she had gone to the coolest amusement park in the world, waited for hours in the line for the biggest roller coaster, and gotten all the way up to the front, only to have the sunburned guy operating the ride tell her that it was out of order, and she couldn't get on. It wasn't fair. They had come so far, only to have the eighth continent taken away from them at the last second.

154

"There is only one explanation," Doctor Grant said. "Something was missing from the compound."

"But how can that be?" Evie asked. "You reassembled the formula. We brought you the other half."

"Most of the work we did years ago was theoretical," Doctor Grant said, pulling a pair of gloves and an empty vial from a drawer under the computer terminal. "The formula was exactly as your father and I had left it when we disbanded the project, but we didn't do extensive testing. Something must be missing." The doctor touched the container to the pool of liquid on the ground, wrinkling his brow as he scooped some up. Suddenly, his expression shifted. "Wait a minute! I've got it. There was an ingredient we talked about incorporating into the formula—a rare fungus called the fecundite mushroom, which grows only in a small island prefecture in Japan."

Evie slapped Rick in the arm. "You hear that? We're going to Japan. We'll be able to get the last component *and* samurai sword souvenirs."

Doctor Grant placed the now-lidded vial by the computer and pulled off his gloves. "Niels Bohr and I will stay here and work on producing a large quantity of the Eden Compound. When you return with the mushrooms, I'll"— he began to singsong—"add it to the batch, and then we will be off to the garbage patch."

"A scientist *and* a poet!" Rick grinned.

Evie shook with excitement. That old feeling of adventure was coming back to her. They were going on another journey.

Rick ran to get their stuff. Evie started to follow, but Doctor Grant added, "Evie, wait. Come here."

"What is it, Doctor Grant?"

He put a comforting hand on her shoulder. "We will make it work. I promise. You'll get your continent. I believe in you."

"You do?"

"There's something about you—it reminds me of your father."

She scratched the back of her head, embarrassed. "Yeah, I get that a lot."

"You are going to need his tenacity, and his creative spirit, to accomplish your mission. Never forget that."

$$\approx\!\!\sim\!\!\sim$$

They parked the *Roost* in a forest on the outskirts of town and ventured into Oshiaka Village. Boxy apartment buildings lined both sides of the street like oversized LEGO structures.

Knowing they were close to their goal, Evie and Rick raced through the town, forcing 2-Tor to hop after them, flapping his metal wings. If only his robot body could have moved as fast as his robot mouth. "First you leave me alone in the *Roost* for over a day. I did not know if you had drowned or abandoned me or what. Now you are leaving me behind! This is highly irregular."

Rick looked around the village suspiciously. "It's weird that there aren't any people out on the street."

"Overzealous construction companies," 2-Tor explained. "They build whole towns prefabricated, but there is no demand, so the completed neighborhoods remain vacant."

"Do you think Condo Corp was behind this place?" Rick asked.

Evie snatched the smartphone from Rick's hand. "Maybe it's a bank holiday. The GPS says we're close. The field where the fecundite mushrooms grow should be just beyond this intersection." She didn't want to think about Vesuvia and her company, not when she could feel their moment of triumph fast approaching. Her sweaty palms tightly gripped the sterile bag they would use to gather the mushrooms. She used to pick dandelions when she went hiking with her dad. This would be no different. The fecundite mushrooms were a bright emerald color—easy to spot.

The Lane siblings rounded the corner and found themselves on the edge of a strip mall. Two lines of storefronts—plastic wig shops, gumdrop emporiums, poodle dry cleaners—surrounded a wide, flat asphalt parking lot. There was not a car in sight.

"Oh, dear," Evie groaned. She ran out into the middle of the lot, which the GPS said was the center of the mushroom field. "This is bad. This is worse than very bad."

"What's wrong?" Rick asked, running over to her.

"Where's the field? Where are the mushrooms?"

A banner hung over one of the store marquees. 2-Tor translated the Japanese characters. "Grand opening! Now with double car capacity."

"Oh no!" Evie wailed. "When they built this shopping mall they must have paved over the field."

"You mean the fecundite mushrooms are under the blacktop?" Rick asked, scraping the asphalt with the toe of his shoe. "How are we going to get to them?"

"I don't know," Evie replied. "Maybe we can find a backhoe or a jackhammer and break up the rock. There must be something we can do. Rick, can you think of anything on the *Roost* that could help us?"

But Rick wasn't listening. His gaze was directed across the parking lot at a stoplight hanging from a wire over the entrance to the mall. A small bird, made of pink plastic, was using it as its perch. It cocked its head to the side and stared at the children.

Then another bird, identical, came out of the sky and landed beside its twin. Then another, and another. A whole flock of the plastic birds landed on the stoplight and its support wire. Their eyes were fixed on Rick and Evie.

"What do they want?" Evie crossed her arms defiantly.

Rick swallowed hard. "I think they want us. Run!"

The birds flapped their wings in computerized unison, rising into the air in a swarm and diving at Rick and Evie.

There was no chance of escape. Sharp plastic beaks pecked at them and pinched their skin. As the birds struck 2-Tor's shell, it sounded like a hailstorm at a car dealership.

The flying pink robots grabbed Rick and Evie by their clothes and hoisted them into the air. The siblings dangled helplessly, kicking their legs. They cried out, but they could not be heard over the noises of the birds, which sounded like a swarm of locusts.

But one sound *could* be discerned over the cacophonous flapping. A giant pink truck rumbled down the street toward them. Its wheels were cylinders, like a steamroller, but a long metal tube came down the front, like the snout of an anteater. As the vehicle came closer, powerful suction snorted the concrete street into its nozzle. The road broke apart in huge chunks, leaving behind dirt and rubble.

Worst of all was who was at the helm. On first look, Evie thought she was seeing things, but a second glance told her that her eyes were indeed telling the truth: Vesuvia Piffle was driving the vehicle. Diana sat behind her, clinging to her seat, looking worried, as usual. They both wore pink hard hats.

The vehicle swerved as Vesuvia stood to wave at them smugly. She cackled like the witch she was. "Thanks for leading me to where the mushrooms grow, Evie LAME. Now *I* have the last component I need to complete the Eden Compound and make the eighth continent my own!"

23

THE LANE GIRL STRUGGLED AGAINST THE PLASTIC BIRDS AS DIANA CHECKED TO MAKE SURE THEY had her locked down tight. The birds had formed chains connecting beak to tail, holding Rick, Evie, and their robot escort fast against the ground. Evie squirmed like an earthworm that had fallen in a can of soda and had to sip her way out. "Let us go!" she screamed.

Vesuvia twirled across the vacant parking lot, sucking on a strawberry-pink lollipop. She struck a ballerina pose and imitated Evie's pleas. "'Let us go! Let us go!' I'll let you go off a *cliff* if you don't shut up."

Diana was glad their mission was almost over. All this flying around the world gave her a tummy ache. "They're all tied up," she told Vesuvia.

Her friend purred. "Oh, Diana. Doesn't it feel good to have everything go pinkly perfect for you? Doesn't it feel grand? Imagine how terrible it would feel to be failures, like these two losers and their robot sparrow."

2-Tor squawked. "I am a crow, young lady."

Vesuvia sneered. "Oh, really? I couldn't tell. You must have been built by a failure."

"Why are you doing this?" Rick struggled against the bird chains.

"Isn't it obvious?" Vesuvia slithered over to Rick, Evie, and 2-Tor.

Diana stepped aside and watched. She felt bad leaving the Lanes helpless like this, but it was the only way to make sure Vesuvia accomplished her goals. Besides, what was the alternative? Overnight Vesuvia had changed Evie into a poisonous toad, to be avoided at school at all costs. Things were worse now. Vesuvia had gone from crazy-sticks-trash-in-your-locker to crazy-ties-you-up-and-leaves-you-to-die. If Diana disobeyed the super-secret CEO of Condo Corp, she would be pinned down just as fast as the Lanes.

She quieted her thoughts and listened to Vesuvia's triumphant monologue. She had rehearsed it all the way from Geneva.

"There was no place on the seven continents where Winterpole and the local authorities would let me build New Miami, my perfect plastic city. But there was another way. An eighth continent—one I could form in my own image."

Evie struggled against her bonds. "The eighth continent is ours! You can't have it."

"Shh . . . shh-shh-shh-shh-shh-shhhh . . ." Vesuvia removed her lollipop and stuck it in Evie's mouth to silence her. Evie gagged and spat out the saliva-covered candy.

"You really are the stupid one, Peevey Evie. If the eighth

continent is yours, why are you tied up in a Japanese parking lot, while I have every last fuddy-duddy mushroom in existence?"

Diana grimaced, glancing at the bag of fungi at her feet. It had not been easy, breaking up the asphalt with the concrete sucker, then foraging in the stiff dirt below for the few shriveled mushrooms that had survived the construction project.

"We've been following you almost from the beginning," Vesuvia explained. "My little bird kept a close eye, so we were always one step behind you, until we found our window to get ahead. And now here we are. Time to leave you in our dust."

"You'll never get away with this!" Evie cried out. "We'll find you."

"Oh, I don't think so." Vesuvia smoothed her shiny plastic hair against her head. "My concrete sucker is going to slurp up all this concrete, and then it's going to slurp up you. Did you know my concrete sucker was manufactured by Lane Industries? How ironic is it that your own father's invention is going to kill you? Hahahahaha! That's hilarious! Enjoy your last few minutes of being a total loser with no taste in clothes."

Vesuvia turned on her plastic heels. Diana hurried to follow. As they passed the concrete sucker, Vesuvia flicked the throttle up to full. Gears roared, and the machine lurched toward the bound Rick, Evie, and 2-Tor.

Diana followed Vesuvia back to her pink hoverjet, leaving the Lanes and their poor robot chaperone to their demise. Vesuvia wasted no time in buckling into her seat in the cockpit and ordering Diana to take off.

"Music, please," Vesuvia commanded once the ship was in the air, and Diana immediately obliged. During the whole ride to the Arctic Sea they blasted the latest album from True North, the world's hottest boy band. Tad Hutstoff was the coolest, and his solos made Diana want to sing out loud. She resisted the urge, however. Vesuvia had made it clear that she thought Diana's singing sounded like a drowning mongoose.

They parked the hoverjet with a splash, just above where the pink bird had told them the submarine lab was hidden. An empty raft of lashed-together plastic bottles floated nearby.

"Diana, you twit, open the torpedo tube."

Frowning sullenly, Diana mumbled, "It's really not nice to talk to me like that. You just have to say please."

Vesuvia scrunched up her face, looking like Diana had insulted her grandmother. "I will talk to you any way I want! I'm the one in charge. Me!"

Diana lowered her head and nodded.

"Now"Vesusiva smoothed her plastic hair against her head,—"deploy Chompedo!"

Something like a giant pink bullet shot from the torpedo tube at the front of the hoverjet. It had the red eyes, dorsal fin, and jagged grin of a bloodthirsty shark.

The pink robo-shark swam in a tight circle around the hoverjet, looking hungry. Diana followed Vesuvia through the top access hatch and watched the shark crash through the waves.

Vesuvia's instructions were somewhat predictable. "Chompedo! Destroy!"

Chompedo jerked his pink metal body sharply, veering onto a collision course with the empty bottle raft. He opened his hydraulic mouth wide, revealing two rows of razor-sharp chainsaw teeth, whirring hungrily.

He didn't need the chainsaws. Chompedo was so big he engulfed the raft in one bite, swallowing it whole. The metal leviathan leaped triumphantly into the air and hit the water with a splash that sent a salty wave crashing down on top of Diana.

Vesuvia was miraculously spared. "Excellent work, Chompedo! You will never fail me. Now come. Let us climb aboard that pretty pink hull of yours. We have work to do."

The robo-shark pulled alongside the hoverjet. Vesuvia and Diana hopped onto his back, the bag of fecundite mushrooms in tow. There was another access hatch that led to a small storage compartment inside Chompedo where the two girls could ride out the journey.

Through the porthole at the front of the compartment, Diana watched as Chompedo dove beneath the waves, speeding them to their destination. Chompedo's red eyes clicked into bright spotlights, which illuminated a long black submarine in front of them.

"Align with that access hatch on the starboard side," Vesuvia ordered.

Chompedo connected the two hatches, forming an airtight entryway.

Vesuvia grinned and twisted open Chompedo's access hatch eagerly. "We are so close, Diana. I can smell it!"

She opened the submarine's hatch, revealing the face of a lonely seal. *"Rowf!"* The seal barked fish breath in Vesuvia's face.

Vesuvia turned green and fell to the floor of the storage compartment with a clang.

"Arf! Arf! Arf!" the seal laughed.

Diana helped her friend to her feet, and together they climbed aboard the sub.

"Now what do we do?" Diana asked, swinging the bag of mushrooms over her shoulder.

Vesuvia scampered ahead, past the sub's darkened laboratories. "Remember what my pink bird told us. This old doctor who helped the Lanes is blind. They were supposed to bring him the febundie mushrooms."

"Fecundite," Diana corrected.

"Fekundun. Felitebrite. Whatever. We give him the mushrooms, he gives us the compound. We just need to pretend to be the Lanes. Should be easy."

Diana wasn't so sure, but Vesuvia had brought her this far. There was no turning back now. They made their way to Doctor Grant's lab, where the old scientist was putting the finishing touches on a big project. Several vats of steaming liquid crossed the middle of the chamber. What looked like giant eggbeaters bobbed in and out of the vats, mixing their contents.

As the girls entered, a long, thin cat sat up on the desk

and hissed at them. Doctor Grant spun around in his chair. His unseeing eyes stared blankly into the darkness. "Quiet, Niels Bohr! Um, hello? Is someone there?"

Vesuvia cleared her throat and spoke with the same energetic twang as Evie Lane. The resemblance was uncanny. "Doctor Grant? It's me, Evie! Rick and I are back with the fedoodoo mushrooms you asked for. Hooray! I did it. I am totally not a loser who would wear shoes from two seasons ago. I'm awesome!"

Doctor Grant showed a relieved smile. "Rick, is this true?"

Diana coughed, trying to make her voice as deep as she could. "Uh, yes! Uh, ahem. Fascinating. Er . . . affirmative. We have the fungal component you requested, Doctor."

"Splendid, just splendid!" Doctor Grant said, holding out his hands. "Give it here."

"Uh, ahem . . . here you go, sir," Diana said, handing over the bag of mushrooms.

The cat—who, upon closer inspection, resembled a tiger—hissed again.

Doctor Grant ignored him and took the bag gratefully. "Rick, you sound funny. Are you all right?"

Diana gulped. Vesuvia gave her a look that could have flayed a fish. Diana tried to laugh. "Huh-huh. Guess so, sir. The water is quite cold."

"Yes, yes, I suppose," Doctor Grant said. "Well, take a seat in the hallway and give me a few minutes. I'll add the mushrooms to the compound so you can be on your way."

"What?!" Vesuvia exclaimed, sounding surprised

that her plan had worked. "Really? Oh, wow bam yippie! Thanks, mister!"

Vesuvia and Diana shuffled out of the room, while Doctor Grant added the mushrooms to the vats. The distillation process did not take long at all. A few minutes later, they were back in the lab. Doctor Grant brought out a pushcart. On it was a machine that looked like a cross between a monster-truck engine and a lawn sprinkler.

"This is my rain machine," Doctor Grant explained. "I've equipped it with a bottle of the condensed Eden Compound. All you have to do is take it to the garbage patch and throw the switch. The compound will disperse into the atmosphere and rain down over the entirety of the garbage patch. And then the eighth continent will be yours!"

"Hooray!" Vesuvia cheered in Evie's voice. "I've never had an accomplishment like this before in my whole life. I wonder what's different about me that it's happening now? Hmm . . ."

"Well, don't wonder too long," Doctor Grant replied, giving the pushcart an extra shove. "You better hurry, or some little snot will try to take the Eden Compound away from you."

Diana coughed. "Ahem. He is right, Ve—uh . . . Evie. We better go."

Silently, Vesuvia stuck a finger in her mouth like she was gagging. "Pleasure doing business with you, Mister Doctor Grant."

They retreated to Chompedo as quickly as they came, dragging the Eden Compound rain machine behind them.

When they were safely back aboard the robo-shark, Vesuvia said, "That was easier than I'd thought! What a blind, old idiot. Chompedo, this smelly old man and his not-pink cat have served their purpose. Once we are away in the hoverjet, you know what to do."

24

RICK FOUGHT AGAINST HIS BONDS, BUT THE CHAINS OF THE ROBOT BIRDS KEPT HIM PINNED TIGHT.

Their plastic wings dug into his skin, leaving red scrapes along his arms and legs.

The concrete sucker roared menacingly as it rumbled toward the helpless children. The nozzle vacuumed up the concrete like dust, crumbling it into nothing as it moved.

2-Tor flailed madly. "This is terrible! Horrible! My date of manufacture is much too recent for me to die."

"2-Tor!" Evie shouted. The birds were chirping so loudly Rick could barely hear her over the noise.

"My circuits cannot take it! I think I leaked some oil. Oh dear oh dear."

"2-Tor!" Evie shouted again. "Will you shut up and listen to me? It's urgent."

The robot hooted. "What could be more urgent than our imminent demise? My only solace is that I will be destroyed along with you both. I could not face your father having failed you so."

"I need you to do something."

2-Tor stopped struggling and gave her a stern look. "Now is certainly not the time."

"Now, I think, is certainly the time!" Rick squirmed frantically. "That machine is gonna get us!"

The concrete sucker inched closer. It was only a few feet away. Rick tried to pull his legs back, but the bird chains had him stuck tight. He shivered at the thought of the concrete sucker overtaking them.

"What can I do?" 2-Tor wailed. "I'm stuck."

"2-Tor! 2-Tor!" Evie said. "I want you to give me a quiz."

"A what?" 2-Tor asked, confused.

"A WHAT?!" Rick screamed. "How is that going to help?"

"A quiz," Evie repeated. "Give us a quiz. Algebra, European history, anything. Please, just please, give us a quiz."

2-Tor grew solemn. "Evelyn, I want you to know that I always thought you failed to value my service as your education augmenter. Now I see that you really do care about your studies, and I am humbled that you would choose to spend your last moments in this life gaining a sliver of knowledge from me."

She glanced at the approaching concrete sucker. "Forget about all that, 2-Tor. Just ask a question."

Rick could feel the hot air of the garbage sucker's nozzle on his toes. "Yeah, she's right. 2-Tor. Quiz us. Hurry!"

2-Tor's body went rigid, and his voice sounded cold and automated. "Quiz administration initiated. Begin comprehension evaluation now. Geography. Children, what is the capital of the United States?"

"New York City!" Evie shouted.

"Incorrect. Complete system shutdown in thirty seconds."

The concrete sucker got closer, and louder.

Evie winced. "Can you make it fifteen seconds?"

2-Tor plowed on. "What is the capital of the United States?"

"Paris!" Rick answered, giving Evie a wink to let her know that he had figured out what she was up to. In spite of their crazy situation, she smiled.

"Incorrect," 2-Tor said. "System shutdown in fifteen seconds."

"Boston! Rome! Montreal!" Evie's voice rose with every word.

"Incorrect. Incorrect. Incorrect. Your performance is shameful, Evelyn. System shutdown in five. Four. Three . . ."

The concrete just beyond Rick's legs broke off and was snorted into the machine. His shoes came off with it. He knew his feet were next so it really didn't matter that he had six changes of sneakers back on the *Roost*.

"Two. One. Engage system shutdown."

2-Tor's crow eyes turned bright red. Electricity surged over his metal exterior, just like it had when the EMP fried his systems back home. The blast cooked the internal computers of the little robot birds pinning them down. The birds fell away like dead insects. An even bigger surge of electricity rushed over the outside of the concrete sucker. The machine smoked and sizzled.

"Come on, run!" Rick brushed away the disabled robot

birds and pulled 2-Tor to his feet with Evie's help. They ran away from the concrete sucker as fast as they could. As they reached the edge of the parking lot, they dove to the ground just before the concrete sucker exploded in a flash of light and rubble.

When the dust settled, Rick and Evie rolled onto their backs and held their bellies, trying to catch their breath. Rick couldn't believe they'd survived.

"Oh my sparks!" 2-Tor said, pressing his wings against the video screen in his belly. A big crack cut diagonally across the glass. "What happened?"

"2-Tor, you are on the fritz!" Evie explained. "When that EMP zapped you, it fried some of your circuits. We brought it out of you when you gave us a quiz back on the *Roost*. You shut the whole tree down, and we almost crashed. I thought that maybe it would work on Vesuvia's birds if I could get you to repeat what happened before."

"A brilliant solution," Rick said, amazed. "Truly, Evie. You saved us. I wish I'd thought of it."

She smiled at him. "Thanks, Rick."

"We need to contact Dad," he added, rising to his feet and dusting himself off. "He'll know what to do."

"But Dad can't use technology," Evie said. "How are we supposed to reach him?"

"Maybe 2-Tor can help. 2-Tor, can you broadcast over the mansion's communication system?"

"I suppose I could," the robot said. "But I am not feeling very top form."

"We just need you to do one more thing, and then back on the *Roost* we will give you the best oil bath of your life."

"Very well," said 2-Tor, who was not a robot to pass up an oil bath. "Initiating communications relay in three, two, one . . ."

Evie called into 2-Tor's speaker box. "Dad! Dad, if you're there, please respond. It's Evie. We've made a lot of progress, but we're in trouble. This girl from our school, Vesuvia Piffle, has stolen the last piece of the Eden Compound. She's going to get the rest from Doctor Grant and take the eighth continent for herself. Dad! Please answer! We need your help to stop her, or we'll lose the continent. Please respond. Please!"

There was no reply.

"Communications relay deactivated," 2-Tor said.

Throwing her hands in the air, Evie groaned, "Now what do we do?"

"Evie, I hate to say it, because you are not going to like it, but I think we need to call Mom."

Evie's voice got dark. "Rick, these words are dread words. They are the second-worst words I have ever heard, a little worse than 'We are all out of ice cream' and not quite as bad as 'You have to go to school on Saturday'. Do we have to?"

Rick nodded. "Yes, we do. Going off again to make the eighth continent. Finding Doctor Grant. Almost dying twice. We have to tell her everything."

"This sounds like a terrible idea," Evie said.

"If Vesuvia is going to take the eighth continent, we'll need Mom's help getting it back."

Evie shrugged. "Okay. 2-Tor, call Mom."

2-Tor's eyes sparked. "Internal database returned zero results for query: Mom. Would you like to search again?"

Evie looked to Rick, puzzled.

Rick slumped down on the curb. "Ugh. That last shock must have corrupted some of his memory. Try her full name. 2-Tor, call Melinda Lane."

"Initiating Internet search for Melinda Lane, CEO of Cleanaspot."

"No, no! Call her. Don't search her."

"Returning 246,108 results. Displaying news stories from the past six hours." The cracked video screen in 2-Tor's stomach brightened, showing a flurry of inexplicable images that made Rick's heart wither.

Rick's mother, in a trim pantsuit, stood on a dais in front of dozens of photographers. The caption read, *Cleanaspot CEO Seals Deal with Winterpole*. She was shaking hands with Diana's mother. They both grinned stupidly, looking like they were thrilled to be there.

"What?!" Evie stammered. "No! This can't be real. Mom is working with Winterpole?"

Rick sounded angry. "2-Tor, give me a veracity check. Where did you acquire this footage?"

"It is available on all business news networks. Such a merger between a corporation and an oversight organization is unprecedented. Usually, Winterpole would veto attempts to form such a merger, but in this case—"

"Winterpole *is* the group merging," Rick finished sourly.

"We can't trust her," Evie said. "Not until we know more about what's going on. She might be helping Vesuvia and Diana as well as Winterpole."

"I hate to say it, but you're right." Rick was so angry he almost didn't notice the tear rolling down Evie's cheek. There had to be a reason for this. He couldn't believe that his mom would sell them out and team up with Winterpole—not after all the work he had done to save the family. How could she do that?

But there was no time to think about this now. Vesuvia was on her way to steal the Eden Compound. They had to race back to the *Cichlid* and warn Doctor Grant before it was too late.

25

EACH HEAVY FOOTFALL ECHOED OFF THE METAL FLOOR AS EVIE AND RICK RACED THROUGH THE submarine to Doctor Grant's lab, calling out his name.

They burst into his lab. The vats of Eden Compound churned noisily.

"I'm right here, children. It's all right."

"Where's the Eden Compound?"

"What do you mean?" Doctor Grant asked. "I gave you a huge vat over an hour ago, when you brought me the fecundite mushrooms."

"Us? That wasn't us. That was our nemesis, Vesuvia Piffle." Evie kicked one of the vats and slumped to the ground in defeat. "Oh, Doctor Grant, she was pretending to be me. If only you weren't blind. If only we had been faster." They were so close, and Vesuvia had snatched the Eden Compound from under their noses.

"BWAHAHAHAHAHAHA!"

Evie looked up, searching for the source of this strange sound.

Doctor Grant leaned back in his chair, slapping his knee, highly amused. "BWAHAHAHA! Oh, Evie, I wish I could see your face. Listen to her, Rick. 'Oh, if only you weren't blind! Boohoohoo.'"

Rick put little effort into hiding his grin.

"What's so funny?" Evie asked, hurt and baffled.

"You think I can't tell the difference between you and some punk pretending to be you? I knew someone was impersonating you the moment she opened her mouth. What a goofus!"

Evie wiped away a tear and smiled. "You mean—"

"You should thank those girls," Doctor Grant said. "They brought us all the fecundite mushrooms we'll need. I distilled them into the compound and loaded the whole thing into this rain machine for dispersal. It's all ready to go."

He wheeled out the rain machine and presented it to her.

"Wow!"

Rick had one last question. "Doctor Grant, if this is the Eden Compound, how did you get Vesuvia and Diana to leave? I can't imagine them just heading out empty-handed."

"I gave them a dispersal device of their own. Oh, I wish I could be there when they use it. And that's not all. I had just enough compound left over to create a little demonstration. Watch this!"

He threw the switch, and the pipes thrummed. In the testing area, the sprinkler opened up over the bag of trash still resting on the bull's-eye. The liquefied compound splattered over the black bag, and suddenly the plastic shimmered into water. The garbage inside crumbled into moist dirt, and little blades of grass sprouted out of it.

"It works! Woohoo! The Eden Compound works!" All of Evie's wishes were coming true. The eighth continent would soon be hers, and she could share it with her family—that is, if they could ever free Dad from his squid-cuff, and if they could figure out what was going on with Mom and Winterpole, and if Rick . . .

Thinking of him, she looked to where he was standing next to her, watching the demonstration of the Eden Compound. His cheeks were red. Tears streamed down his face.

"Rick! What is it? What's wrong?"

"Nothing . . ." he said. "It's beautiful. I can't believe it. You were right. I see it now. Evie, you were right. We can build the eighth continent. There are so many possibilities. It's almost real. It's going to happen."

"It is," Evie said. She couldn't stop smiling. "Oh, Rick. Doctor Grant. We're going to make a continent!"

"We certainly are," agreed Doctor Grant.

Evie felt a wave of relief wash over her. After all the danger they had faced in Japan, all the heartbreak with her mother. Finally, the Eden Compound was in her hands. Finally, things were starting to go right.

And then something slammed into the side of the sub.

The old metal hull groaned in agony, rolling onto its port side. Evie tumbled into the wall. Rick crashed against the hard surface beside her. Doctor Grant slipped out of his chair and hit the floor with a yelp.

The rain machine slid down the steep slope of the floor, careening toward Rick.

Evie grasped him by both arms and rolled him on top of her, just before the machine slammed into the wall beside them, hitting the spot where Rick had been sprawled out a second before.

"Whoa! That was close. I owe you." Rick looked like he was dreaming with his eyes open.

"Don't get mushy about it," Evie replied, pushing him off her.

They scrambled to their feet. "What *was* that?" Evie asked.

"I have no idea," Doctor Grant said. "But I think we should get out of here as fast as possible. Come on, Niels Bohr. Let's go."

Something slammed into the sub again, this time with a bang that made Evie's ears feel like they were going to pop off.

Then the impossible happened. An enormous pink robo-shark burst through the wall of the lab. Chainsaw teeth whirred violently as the shark flew across the room.

The shark tore through the far wall and out into the sea, cutting a path clear through the sub. Evie had no time to process this before a column of salt water surged into the lab, flooding the room.

Evie clutched the Eden Compound. Rick clutched Evie. Doctor Grant clutched Niels Bohr. And then wet darkness swallowed them all.

26

"PREFABRICATED HOUSING READY TO DEPLOY, ADMIRAL PIFFLE!"

The deep voice came clear over the radio on the bridge of Vesuvia's double-decker yacht. Crewmen ran from station to station, preparing for what their boss had declared would be the sight of a lifetime: the creation of a new continent.

Diana also felt a pinch of excitement. It hadn't been easy acquiring the Eden Compound, and the measures they had taken to get it were morally questionable, to say the least. But now their quest was over, and the entire Condo Corp navy had shown up to accelerate the construction of New Miami.

From the admiral's chair, which looked like it belonged on a starship except for the pink pleather cushions, Vesuvia pulled the microphone close to her over-glossed lips. "Stand by, Captain Blusterphoon! We are starting the continent-creation process now."

The time had come. Diana followed Vesuvia out of the main cabin. The wretched stench of the garbage patch hit them immediately, making Diana's hair go flat. Vesuvia covered her nose and mouth with the collar of her pink plastic jacket.

She led Diana down a spiral staircase, past the in-ground swimming pool, to the yacht's aft balcony, where technicians were powering up the rain machine. It was hard to believe that the push of a button could remove so much trash and waste from the world and put an entire new landmass in its place.

Diana felt proud to be in on the ground floor of a new continent. She wondered what it would look like. Would it resemble Old Miami? Palm trees and beaches? Or green fields and sharp mountain peaks, like back home in Switzerland? She couldn't wait to find out.

Not that it would matter for very long. As soon as the continent was made, Vesuvia would go to work blasting it, paving it, and reshaping it to her liking.

The other ships of the Condo Corp fleet pulled into a tight formation around Vesuvia's yacht. There were tankers to carry oil, fresh water, and Vesuvia's favorite pink soda. There were freighters to transport the prefab houses, apart-ment buildings, smoothie stands, and asphalt pavers. And of course, surrounding the other vessels, there were security frigates to keep Vesuvia's most precious cargo safe.

Rumors of the mysterious device that would make New Miami possible had spread from ship to ship. Every sailor in the fleet wanted to see the Eden Compound do its work.

Diana included herself in that group. As the technicians stepped back from the rain machine, she hurried forward and lifted the plastic casing that covered the activation plunger. It had a T-shaped handle, like the kind on TNT detonators in old cartoons. She wrapped her hands around the plunger's crossbar and started to raise it.

"HEY!" Vesuvia screeched. "I said, 'HEY!' That's my Eden Compound. That's my rain machine. And that's my job! Get away from that thing."

Disappointed, Diana let go of the plunger and backed away from the rain machine. "You can ask nicely, Vesuvia. You can say please."

"Please. Don't be such a spoiled brat, Diana." Vesuvia tiptoed over to the machine, singing a little song she had composed for this occasion. "Everywhere I go, they say I'm the best CEO. I have right here in my hand the power to create a sweet new land!"

She grabbed the plunger and raised it to its full height. Gritting her teeth, Vesuvia pushed down with all her strength.

A green mist sprayed into the air, hitting Vesuvia full in the face. She collapsed to the deck of the yacht, choking and clawing at her skin. It only took a second for Diana to understand why.

The most horrific stench washed over her, like the body odor of an anti-shower activist who'd just run a half marathon while eating a tuna fish and Limburger cheese salad, like egg stew cooked in a garbage bag and left in a public bathroom to marinate, like—Diana hated to admit it—her gym socks.

Fortunately, Diana had only inhaled the stench

secondhand. Vesuvia had gotten a blast of it up her nostrils, mainlining the wretched stink directly to her brain. She screeched, "BWAGH! Skunk spray! It tastes like a yellow fart!"

Diana covered her face to try to block out the smell— but also to keep Vesuvia from seeing her laugh.

The technicians and other crew members looked on with befuddled disappointment. They had come to see a new continent get built, not their boss roll around like a lunatic.

"Turn this boat around!" Vesuvia shrieked. "The whole fleet. Get clear of the garbage patch! We are victims of a cruel prank."

The engines started up, grinding against the fishing line and plastic wrappers floating in the water. Even when Vesuvia's face was green with skunk spray, the Condo Corporation did not question orders from the boss.

Vesuvia eventually fumbled her way to the swimming pool and threw herself in, fully dressed, to clean up. When she emerged, dripping and furious, Diana was waiting with a towel.

"Those nasty Lanes have pulled a trick on us," Vesuvia spoke venomously. "And that nasty blind doctor. I bet even his stupid tiger cat had something to do with it! But don't worry, Diana. It's not over yet. We just need to wait. One day, the Lanes will cut it a little too close, and then I will have my revenge!"

27

VOID.

TO RICK IT MEANT COLD. DARKNESS. EMPTINESS.

It meant the opposite of anything.

His hair swirled around his muted ears in the big dark-blue expanse. He was not sure how many minutes he'd gone without air, but after a while, he stopped screaming bubbles, and nothing came out.

A heavy arm buckled around his deflated chest and pulled, plucking him from the submerged lab like a rabbit from a hat.

He broke the surface in a spray of inhaled water. The ceiling of the laboratory was only inches from his clogged nose.

"Rick! RIIIIICK!" he heard his sister scream.

Doctor Grant still had his arms around him. "He's all right. Rick, you're alive. Come on. Swim. Swim for your life!"

The lights on the sub had all gone out. It was pitch dark. Fortunately, Doctor Grant was quite familiar with navigating the *Cichlid* in complete darkness. They formed a train and swam through the giant hole the robo-shark had punched in the wall, back into the hallway. Any chance they had to save the formula for the Eden Compound vanished when they left that room. Even if Rick's hard drive had survived being drowned, he would never be able to find it.

The air pocket at the top of the chamber allowed them to breathe between deep swims through the tunnels of the sub. But there wasn't a second to spare. The sub was sinking. If they did not get to the airlock and escape in a few minutes, they were done for.

At the end of the hallway, Doctor Grant felt for a hatch in the ceiling. "Rick, Evie, help me open this."

It took their combined strength to turn the wheel and push open the heavy metal hatch. Doctor Grant boosted Rick into the next hallway first, then Rick turned around and pulled Evie up beside him. Working as a team they managed to get Doctor Grant through the hatch, splashing water into the dry hallway. When he cleared the hatch, they slammed it shut.

"Now what?" Rick asked, gasping for breath. His heart beat heavily in his chest, like he was down to half a life container.

"This way looks clear," Evie said, starting down the hall toward the rear of the ship.

"No, no!" Doctor Grant shouted. "That leads to the volcano engine room. We can't go through there." He led them the other way down the hall, pointing toward a much bigger access hatch at the far end, this one on the wall. "This next room should be safe."

The wheel was almost impossible to turn. Rick gritted his teeth and imagined the wheel was that robo-shark's pink neck. He felt his muscles flex, and the wheel gave, spinning wildly out of control.

"That did it!" Doctor Grant managed to say before the door flew open and a tidal wave greeted them. The water scooped them up and carried them back the way they had come. Rick scraped his back against the first hatch they had opened. He tried to grab something, but the current was too strong. Rick, Evie, and Doctor Grant tumbled straight toward the volcano engine room, clawing for a handhold and failing to find purchase.

"This way!" Doctor Grant shouted, pulling them into the room, which was scorching hot, even surrounded by all this arctic water.

"But you said *don't* go in this room," Rick reminded him.

"No choice now," the doctor explained. "But I built it. I'll keep you safe."

A thin layer of water covered the floor of the engine room. Some of the glass chambers were cracked. Rubble blocked off the passageways between them.

For a moment, it was quiet. Maybe the damage to the sub had shut down the engine.

The familiar hum-whine of the engine powering up put an answer to that question. In the chamber in front of them, the valve opened. The box filled with molten light.

In a flash the light was gone. The water on the floor had

vaporized, and the water outside the chamber rushed in to fill the empty space.

"We gotta go in there," Doctor Grant said. "It's the only way through."

"Go in there?!" Evie asked in disbelief before Rick could say the same thing. Doctor Grant wanted them to enter the chamber where a blast of thermal death had been seconds earlier.

"I know the pattern," he explained. "Hurry!"

Shaking with fright, Rick followed Doctor Grant, who boldly ventured into the chamber. His feet sizzled as the superheated floor boiled the water on the bottom of his sneakers, then melted the rubber of his soles. Walking felt like he had stepped in a steak-sized wad of masticated chewing gum.

The whole sub shook, buckling under the strain of the water. Machinery shifted out of place and broke loose. Nuts and bolts fell from the ceiling. A loose girder toppled to the ground.

They reached the far side of the chamber and cleared the box. As they waited in the narrow gap between the rooms, to time their next move and to catch their breath, the valve opened up again. The chamber behind them flooded with heat. The blast pushed the trio against the far wall. Rick smelled something awful, and he clutched his arm, realizing the heat had singed off all his arm hair.

"Now! Next room!" Doctor Grant barked, pulling Rick and Evie with him.

They ran across the chamber as fast as they could, struggling to stay on their feet as the sub shook beneath them. Above, the valve started to open when they were halfway across the chamber.

"Doctor!" Rick cried out, alarmed.

"Move!" the doctor yelled, and they dove through the small opening at the far end of the room.

The heat came down just behind them. Rick saw spots as the light hit his eyes.

Doctor Grant held Rick and Evie tightly. "There's just one more, and we're through!"

Rick could see the door on the far side of the room, beyond the last chamber. Through the door and down the hall was the airlock where they had entered the submarine. If they could just reach that airlock, they could escape.

"Now's our chance. Run!" Doctor Grant shoved Rick from behind, pushing him into the chamber.

Startled, Rick ran as fast as he could until he reached the other end. He slipped out the far side and turned to catch his breath, relieved that he was safe. Doctor Grant came next, followed by Evie, but the sub shuddered, and a bundle of steel girders broke loose above them and toppled into the chamber.

Evie screamed as they landed on top of her, knocking her off her feet and pinning her to the ground.

"Evie!" Rick screamed, running back into the chamber.

Doctor Grant grabbed him from behind and pulled with surprising strength, hurling Rick away from danger.

Rick crashed into the wall. He tried to gasp for breath, but his wind was gone.

Rick watched helplessly as Doctor Grant crawled back into the chamber and pulled on the fallen girders with all his strength.

"Get back!" Evie shouted. "We're both going to die."

"No, you're not," the doctor grunted, throwing off another girder. He pulled her free, just as the valve started to open.

Rick strained against the pain. "*Hrk!* Run!"

They ran. At the last second Doctor Grant shoved Evie with both hands, sending her tumbling out of the chamber, just as it filled with light. Evie was facedown on the floor, but Rick watched helplessly as the lava machine consumed its inventor. Through the bright glow, Rick could see nothing but a shadow, and when the chamber cleared, Doctor Grant was gone. Not an ash or cinder remained.

"No!" Evie screamed, running back to the chamber. "Where is he? Where did he go? Where?"

"Evie!"

"He was right behind me. He had to get out. He had to."

"Evie!" Rick begged.

"I don't understand where he went."

Rick pulled her toward him. "Evie, he's gone. We have to go. Please!"

In a stupor, Evie followed her brother. He guided her out of the engine room and up the hall, to the room with the airlock. Evie was babbling about Doctor Grant, so Rick closed them inside the room with the very agitated seal.

Rick threw the switch to open the submarine. Like there were not enough holes in it already.

"Get ready to swim!" The chamber filled with water, and the airlock popped open.

Evie, Rick, and a frightened seal were sucked out like they were being flushed down the toilet. Rick took his sister in his arms and kicked for the surface.

They came up, gasping desperate breaths. Rick's teeth chattered at the shock of going from the heat of the engine room to the cold of the ocean. He fumbled for his phone with numb fingers and activated the homing beacon.

After a few seconds, the *Roost* appeared overhead and landed in the water a short distance off. He could see 2-Tor inflating the rescue raft to come pick them up.

Rick had never been a strong swimmer, but he managed to tread water and hold Evie above the surface. "Are you okay?" he asked his sister. He could not account for all the salt water on her face.

"I didn't even get to say goodbye. And it was my fault he had to come back."

Rick held her tighter than he had since they were babies. He didn't know how to tell her that no one blamed her for what happened, not even Doctor Grant. The look on the old man's face as he pushed Evie to safety had said everything. He knew what was going to happen the moment he went back into the chamber, and he was at peace with it.

The only parties responsible for what happened were that robo-shark and its owner. He would not let Evie blame herself.

But how to recover? Everything had been on the sub, and the sub was lost.

SPWOOOOOSH!

Rick and Evie whipped their heads around at the noise. The rain machine floated on the surface a few feet away, surrounded by inflatable yellow buoys. The canister of Eden Compound was still in place.

And to Rick's great relief, riding atop the machine was one very soggy Niels Bohr.

The water had soaked him skinny, and droplets dripped from his whiskers. He meowed his anger and sorrow, but he quieted when the children swam over to him and smoothed out his coat, telling him he was safe.

They still had the cat, and they still had the Eden Compound, which meant the dream of the eighth continent was still alive. Now, more than ever, they had to make it real, for Doctor Grant and for the world.

THE *ROOST* FLEW LOW OVER THE OCEAN, KICKING UP A TRAIL OF SHIPPING POPCORN AND SOUP CAN lids as it crossed the Great Pacific Garbage Patch.

Evie looked out the cockpit window, her eyes narrow and her lips tight. After what had happened to Doctor Grant, she was ready to see the garbage patch destroyed.

"Okay, 2-Tor, bring us in for a landing over there." Rick pointed to the remnants of several box spring mattresses floating on a bed of plastic bags.

The *Roost* set down with a splash and bobbed among the garbage like a carrot in some very unappetizing dip.

Rick wheeled the rain machine around and pulled it into the hall.

"Shall I stand guard here again, Richard?" asked 2-Tor.

"No way. You've been a big part of this adventure. You should be there to watch it end. Niels Bohr can hold down the fort. Right, Niels Bohr?"

The tiger cat leaped on top of the control console and sprawled out on the dashboard.

"See? He'll be fine."

Evie knew that wasn't true. How could Niels Bohr be fine? Evie wasn't fine, and she'd only known Doctor Grant a couple of days. Of course, Niels Bohr had been able to get out of the submarine on his own, and save the Eden Compound, without getting his friend killed.

"Evie?"

She turned to her brother. "Sorry, Rick. Did you say something?"

"We've come so far. It's time to make that continent."

Rick, Evie, and 2-Tor made their way to the bottom level of the *Roost*, where the internal power plant chugged like a marching band, pistons firing. Evie shivered. Even though the engine room was one of her favorite places on the ship, being there felt eerily similar to being back on the submarine.

It seemed to Evie that no matter what she did, she couldn't escape the bad memories. They hadn't even had time to deflate the big life raft that 2-Tor had picked them up in back in the Arctic Sea.

Now the birdbot stumbled in while Rick and Evie carefully lowered the rain machine into the rubber boat. Evie hit the button on the wall, and the gate of thick bark rumbled open. She didn't want to get back in the boat, but she forced herself to hop in as Rick lowered the onboard motor into the water, and they sputtered away from the *Roost*.

The motor had a lot of trouble cutting through the trash-filled water of the garbage patch. Several times Rick and Evie had to attack the jammed propeller with oars, untangling fishing lines and shopping bags.

From her vantage point in the middle of the garbage patch, down low, on the surface, Evie concluded that the term "continent" was well deserved. Trash went as far as the eye could see in every direction. The only seabirds were the dead ones floating in the water, choked on those plastic rings soda cans came attached to. It was a desolate, horrible world, one without interest in supporting life.

"It's a graveyard," Evie said, feeling sick.

Rick wrenched his face. "Endless ranks of the dead would smell better than this place."

They found a clearing in the blanket of trash, a small pool of black water where the raft fit snugly. "This looks as good a place as any," Rick said. "Let's power up the machine."

Evie switched on the device, trying not to inhale too deeply. She never thought to ask Doctor Grant if the Eden Compound would remove the gross stench of trash as part of transforming its substance. Now she never could.

But she'd know the answer soon enough.

"Activating internal battery now," Rick said, flipping a switch on the bottom of the rain machine. It hummed to life, illuminating the few dozen lights that surrounded the activation plunger on top of the machine.

"Are you ready?" Evie asked, placing her hand on the plunger.

"Are you?" Rick smiled, placing his hand over hers.

"Children," 2-Tor interrupted, putting a sudden stop to their moment of triumph.

They froze and looked at their robot guardian. "What is it?" Rick asked.

The robot's voice was cold. "Children, it is time for a quiz."

Rick and Evie shared a worried look. "Uh, 2-Tor," Rick said, "I thought that last shock fried your quiz software."

"Children, it is time for a quiz."

Evie gave her brother a nudge. "Something's wrong with him."

"I can see that," Rick agreed.

2-Tor shouted so loudly that they jumped back from the rain machine. "Answer my quiz, or you will be grounded for the rest of your natural lives!"

Evie reached for the plunger. "I'm just going to activate the machine and not deal with this right now."

"No, wait," Rick said. "He might interfere if we don't do what he says. And this is all the Eden Compound there is. We only get one shot at using it. It's not worth the risk."

Evie sighed, taking a step away from the machine. "Okay, 2-Tor, fine. Quiz time. Let's go."

"Zoology. What is your favorite animal?"

"Excuse me?"

"Where is the best pizza in Uzbekistan? How many giraffes fit in a jar of peanut butter? Who discovered the color blue?"

Evie rolled her eyes. "I don't know, 2-Tor. Pork?"

"Incorrect! Incorrect! Your failure indicates that you must repeat the fourth grade."

"But I'm in *fifth* grade," Evie snapped.

"This is very bad," Rick said, moving to the robot's side.

"Understatement!" Evie said, hugging herself.

As Rick reached to adjust 2-Tor's machinery, the robot threw out his wings to their full span, blocking out the sun. He screeched, sounding like a cross between a hawk and television static.

The cracked screen in 2-Tor's chest went bright white, and then a face appeared.

Their mother's.

"Multi-way communication channel opened," 2-Tor said.

"Well, well, well," their mother hissed. "If it isn't my little embarrassments. You thought you could break every rule imaginable and get away with it? No one disrespects me like that. This is UN-AC-CEPTABLE!"

Evie's heart fell. "But, Mom! We can explain."

"Uh-uh. No need for that. I found that message you left for your father at the house. Eden Compounds. Eighth continents. I am ashamed of you."

"Don't speak to us that way," Rick said, glaring at 2-Tor's screen.

"I'm your mother, Richard. I will speak to you any way I choose. And really, I expect this kind of behavior from your stupid sister, but not from you, dear."

"Mom!" Evie cried. "How can you say that?"

"Let's be honest," her mother continued. "These latest shenanigans are only the most recent in a long string of disappointments."

"But we succeeded!" Evie said. "I accomplished something. Isn't that what you're always criticizing me for? Never accomplishing anything?"

"What exactly have you achieved?" The image of her mother shook with static, then reappeared, looking more judgmental than ever.

Evie felt a warmth inside of her, a passion that had been smoldering for a long time and suddenly burst into flames. She felt it at the sight of all the garbage creeping up on their boat, and at the thought of the death of her friend Doctor Grant, which weighed like a squid-cuff on her back. It was the contempt on her mother's glitchy face that finally pushed Evie to *make* something of herself. The continent was more important than her needs now. It was bigger than her family. Bigger than any one person. Her mom needed to see how close they were to changing the world—to saving it.

"We have the Eden Compound, Mother. Now we can terraform the garbage patch into the eighth continent."

"Yes, yes, make the continent, free your father. I've heard enough of it. Evie, your father doesn't need help. I took care of that by teaming up with Winterpole. He won't be going to the Prison at the Pole, thanks to me. Not you."

"It's not about that!" Evie said. "It's what we set out to do, but it isn't what we needed to do. Don't you see, Mom? This planet is sick. There is pollution everywhere, and it's killing the world. Animals are dying. Look at this water! It's black, Mom. Water isn't supposed to be black."

"I don't see what this has to do with—"

"You run Cleanaspot! You should understand. We are trying to clean up the world. Building the eighth continent is a big step toward making that happen."

"No one cares about the eighth continent," her mother

sneered.

Evie pointed a finger at the screen. "You told me to make something of myself. I'm trying to make you proud of me."

"Well, you're not. And now you're bringing your brother into it. Rick, you must see that your sister is crazy. Put a stop to this at once. Come home."

A strange look passed over Rick's features. He looked determined, resolute. His face then shifted again, like the forced expressions of a robot. He looked angry.

"Mother is right, Evie," he said. "You have screwed it all up again."

"Rick, what are you saying?"

"I hate you! You are lazy, and you disgust me. I never wanted to come on this trip, but you were too lazy and stupid to do it alone. You needed me."

Evie felt like her insides were spilling out. "Stop saying these things."

Her mother cackled. "No, Richard! Keep going!"

"We should have listened to Mom. Who cares about Dad? We should have stayed home and played video games."

"Yes! That's right!" Mom said.

"We should have left the eighth continent alone."

"No!" Evie said.

"Yes! Yes! Yes!" her mother said.

"Evie, you are stupid," Rick said.

"She is!" her mother agreed.

"We should have turned the eighth continent into New Miami!"

"Exactly! That was my idea," Mom said.

Evie was stunned. "Wait, what?"

"Wait, what?" Mom asked, quite surprised and sounding embarrassed.

"Aha!" Rick cried out. "I knew it was you, Vesuvia."

Their mother screamed and dissolved into a flurry of static, revealing the bright pink face of Vesuvia Piffle. "You tricked me!" she squeaked.

"You tried to trick us first." Rick turned to his sister. "I'm sorry, Evie. I didn't mean any of those things I said before. I was trying to get Vesuvia to blow her cover."

Evie collapsed in the raft. She was glad that Vesuvia had been found out and that Rick and her mother were not really being so dreadful to her, but she didn't know how much more heart strain she could take. She was used to physical challenges, not emotional ones.

"That's right. My little pink birds told me all about the drama between you two. But that doesn't matter now," Vesuvia said. "It's already too late. Look behind you."

A fleet of ships was cutting through the garbage on a direct course with them. A squad of speedboats had been dispatched to disable the *Roost*, while the rest were coming for the raft with the Eden Compound. At the bow of the lead yacht stood Vesuvia and Diana, holding computer tablets. Vesuvia hurled hers into the water, and the image on 2-Tor's stomach cut out.

"I say," 2-Tor announced, "why do I suddenly feel the urge to go shopping?"

Vesuvia screamed across the water. "It's too late, Lanes. I'm back, and now the Eden Compound will be mine!"

29

VESUVIA'S SHIPS WERE GETTING CLOSER TO THE RAFT. RICK AND EVIE ONLY HAD A MOMENT BEFORE they arrived.

Rick knew he had to make sure Evie understood why he'd said those things. "Evie, listen to me. Vesuvia used 2-Tor to impersonate Mom. She was trying to get us to fight each other. I didn't mean what I said. Please, forgive me for being so terrible."

"It's okay," she said. "I have been pretty stupid this whole journey."

"That's not true. You've been smart, and very brave. I don't even remember how many times you have saved my life, and you know how good I usually am with numbers."

"But Doctor Grant—"

"Believed in our mission. Because of you. Because of what you said. Now we have to make him proud."

Evie's head and heart had seemed heavy ever since they'd left the Arctic, but as Rick said this, he watched his sister perk up and brighten.

Then Vesuvia arrived and ruined the good mood. Her yacht bumped into the raft. From their place at the bow, Diana looked on while Vesuvia spat at Rick and Evie. "Well, if it isn't my two least favorite fashion disasters. I have good news! You are going to be the first visitors to New Miami. Doesn't that sound exciting?"

2-Tor pointed a sharp wing at her. "Young lady, you leave these children alone or else."

Vesuvia laughed. "Or else what? What will you do? Rust on me? Hahahahaha!"

2-Tor lowered his wings helplessly.

Evie glared. "You are not getting the Eden Compound, Vesuvia. No matter what."

"But New Miami will be so much fun!" Vesuvia declared. "There will be ten-story arcades for Rick and all sorts of fun stuff for you, Evie. Paintball, ropes courses, climbing walls, wind surfing. New Miami will be way cooler than Trash Island."

"We are trying to build an eighth continent!" Evie said.

"Yes, I know. You thought you could build your own eighth continent to get away from me and all the cool, wonderful girls at ISES. But now that continent is *mine*. Oh, I think I might force you to live with me in New Miami, so I can torment you every single day. Won't that be your worst nightmare?"

Evie scoffed. "You are so narrow-minded. Sure, I started off this journey trying to make the continent for my own reasons, but it's bigger than me now. So your petty meanness doesn't hurt me at all. I couldn't care less what you and the kids at school think of me. I'm building the continent for something greater."

"Continent, schmontinent. You're not going to be building anything. Diana called her mommy. Winterpole agents are on their way, and won't they be surprised to see all the rules you two have been breaking on behalf of your criminal father?"

"We haven't broken any more rules than you!" Rick said. While they bickered, he tried to get a sense of the odds stacked against them. It did not look good. Vesuvia's fleet had dozens of ships, and she had hundreds of grown-up crew members at her command. Even the *Roost* was surrounded by her boats.

Vesuvia stretched like a triumphant lioness, her plastic clothes squeaking. "I hear the penalty for aiding a known criminal is quite severe. Perhaps you will be sent to the Prison at the Pole along with your father. But I'll tell you what. If you give me the Eden Compound, I'll call off Winterpole and save your family."

At a time like this, when the odds were so clearly not in their favor, and their futures were at such risk, part of Rick wanted to agree. He could not bear to see Evie or his dad go to the Prison at the Pole. But he knew his sister would never back down and never surrender. He waited to see what she decided.

Vesuvia extended a perfectly manicured hand. "So, do we have a deal?"

Evie was still full of surprises, even sad ones. "It's a deal."

Vesuvia clapped like she was watching the world's most interesting golf tournament. "Oh, goodie! Diana, lower the bridge."

Diana and a couple crewmen fetched a boarding ramp and lowered it into the raft.

"Are you sure about this?" Rick whispered to Evie in the bustle.

Evie frowned. "No, but we don't have a choice. We can't risk our family's future. What good would the eighth continent be if I lost you and Mom and Dad?"

Any further conversation was interrupted as the crewmen grabbed Rick and Evie roughly by the arms and dragged them aboard Vesuvia's yacht. The others carried the rain machine on their shoulders and set it down at Vesuvia's feet like a prize catch.

"Excellent!" she squealed. "Excellent. This is wonderful! Diana, give me my phone."

Diana scowled. "Vesuvia, for the last time, don't talk to me like that."

Vesuvia gave her a look that made Diana's scowl look like a smile. "I'll talk to you any way I feel like. Sheesh, Diana. Stop it. No one likes a bossypants. Now, hand me my stupid phone!"

Looking miserable, Diana gave Vesuvia the device.

Vesuvia dialed a number, winking at Evie. "Hello? Mister Snow? Yes, it's me. I have Rick and Evie Lane in custody. Winterpole may commence with the siege and arrest them."

Dozens of Winterpole hoverships came out of the sky, swooping toward the fleet like birds of prey that had just found their latest meal.

"What?!" Evie launched herself at Vesuvia, breaking free of the crewmen and tackling the girl flat. Her phone went flying. Evie grabbed her by her plastic lapels and shook her. "You promised! You went back on your word."

Rick thought Vesuvia was crying in pain, but actually she was laughing. Between fits of giggles, she said. "Stupid Evie! You're so, so stupid!"

The crewmen ripped Evie off Vesuvia and pinned her to the ground.

Evie screamed into the deck of the ship. "You promised! You liar!"

A hovership slowed to a stop a few feet above the water, with a good vantage point over the yacht. The side door of the hovership slid open, revealing the smartly dressed figure of Mister Snow.

"Good afternoon," he said professionally. "Young Mister and Miss Lane. I regret to inform you that you are under arrest. I will now escort you to the Prison at the Pole."

30

EVIE WASN'T SURE WHICH WAS WORSE, THE FACT THAT SHE WAS SURROUNDED BY WINTERPOLE agents, or that Vesuvia had her dirty hands on the Eden Compound.

Over by the *Roost*, the Winterpole agents Barry and Larry fired a glue cannon at her beloved hovership. A spiderweb of blue glue held the *Roost* in the water. There was no way it could take off.

"Hold still!" Barry cheered, squeezing his glue-cannon trigger like it owed him money.

"Still needs some work," Larry said, referring to his partner's latest catchphrase.

Evie pleaded with her captor. "Mister Snow, wait. I thought you said that because we're kids we can't be sent to the Prison at the Pole."

The Winterpole officer looked down his nose at her. "Due to certain circumstances, the director has made an exception, which I will explain in due time."

Vesuvia glared at all of them. "Don't explain it. Hurry

205

up! Get these criminals out of my sight. I have business to attend to."

Mister Snow pulled out a tablet and scrolled to the appropriate section of the document on his screen. "Winterpole Statute 19-W3 insists that I read the complete list of infractions before the violator can be taken into custody. Please allow me to start from the beginning."

"Oh, here we go," Evie said, rolling her eyes.

Mister Snow began to read. "The accused Richard Lane and the accused Evelyn Lane are guilty of the following infractions. Entering Winterpole Headquarters without the proper permission slip. Requesting a permission slip to enter Winterpole Headquarters without the proper permission slip. Littering in Winterpole Headquarters lobby. Inappropriately hostile communication with a Winterpole officer. Accessing Winterpole mission database without permission. Accessing Winterpole personnel database without permission. Attempting to alter Winterpole personnel database without permission . . ."

Vesuvia stomped her foot. "By the ghost of Chanel, will you hurry up?!"

Mister Snow lowered his eyes at her. "I most certainly will not hurry up, miss. Winterpole Statute 19-W3 insists—"

"Fine, fine!" she said. "Ugh. This is taking forever."

In reality, it took twenty minutes to complete the list of infractions. During that time, the hot Pacific sun drenched them all in sweat, and the reek from the garbage surrounding the ships made Evie's head spin.

Mister Snow took a deep breath to finish reading the

infractions. "The accused Evelyn Lane made a sarcastic comment in reference to the reading of charges. Quote: 'Oh, here we go.' The accused Evelyn Lane also rolled her eyes. And finally, the crime that will finally allow me to send you to the Prison at the Pole, seventy-two minutes ago, the father of the accused violated his house arrest and exited Lane Mansion."

Evie and her brother exchanged a glance. Their father exited Lane Mansion? Dad was on the loose?

Mister Snow pointed at Rick and Evie. "Fit these two for squid-cuffs."

Two Winterpole agents reached into buckets and pulled out a pair of the writhing cyber squids.

Evie didn't care about that. Her father had escaped! That could only mean one thing. She watched the sky.

An enormous flock of birds soared overhead. At the center of the flock was a grand hovership shaped like a bird with outstretched wings.

"Dad!" Evie cheered at the sight of her father's personal supership.

The *Drongo* did a barrel roll, then swooped low over Vesuvia's yacht, upside down. Everyone hit the deck, literally, except for Evie, who stood, cheering happily. As the *Drongo* passed by, she saw into the domed glass cockpit. Her mother sat at Dad's side. She was smiling and waving at her.

So it was true. The deal her mom had made with Winterpole was just another one of Vesuvia's ruses.

While the *Drongo* came around for another pass, Vesuvia

and her crew, the Winterpole agents, and Rick stood back up, right in time for the Lane family's bird collection to say an up close and personal hello.

The birds swarmed the deck like a plague of locusts.

Vesuvia screamed. "Ew! Birds are smelly! Yuck! Get them away! Get them out of my hair! Diana, help meeeeeee!"

Mister Snow waved to his agents. "Everyone, get back to the hoverships. Retreat!"

Many of the birds were drawn to the shiny exterior of their old friend 2-Tor, and they perched on his shoulders just like they did back home.

In the chaos, Evie found Rick, who like herself was being ignored for a moment. "Rick! Now's our chance! We have to activate the rain machine."

"Yes!" Rick cheered. "Eden Compound, here we come!"

They ran across the deck of the yacht to where the rain machine was guarded—or, rather, would have been guarded if a family of parakeets wasn't trying to start a nest in the guard's hair.

Standing on opposite sides of the rain machine, Rick and Evie shared an almost giddy look. "Go on, push it!" Rick said.

"You do it," Evie said. "You've had to put up with me this whole time."

"How about together?"

They placed their hands on the plunger's crossbar. Then, together, they pushed down, activating the rain machine and starting the release of the Eden Compound.

Rick and Evie were knocked to the ground as a geyser of

iridescent green liquid shot out of the rain machine. It went high, impossibly high, high as the clouds.

The Eden Compound-infused rain came down from the sky in a torrent of what looked like lime soda. It covered everything, the hoverships and the fleet of boats, the birds, the people, and, of course, the garbage.

The effect was immediate. Plastic bags sprouted moss. Warped sheet metal crumbled into dirt. An old Styrofoam ice chest blossomed into a huge flower with white petals.

Evie's heart soared. It worked!

The Eden rain spattered Vesuvia, soaking her beloved pink plastic jacket. The jacket ballooned in size, turned dark brown, and oozed across her skin. Now it was mud.

"Ew! Revolting!" she yelled. She tried to wipe the mud away, but her hand touched something slimy. "YAAGH! GET IT OFF!" she screamed the second she saw what was in her hand. Her mud jacket was crawling with worms and spiders.

Mister Snow and the agents of Winterpole continued their retreat to their hoverships. They started to take off, but when the Eden Compound–infused rain fell on the vehicles, the metal hulls sprouted so much grass they looked like furry flying ducks. The interiors of the hoverships moistened into soil; the electronics twisted into brambles. By the time the ships hit the water, they had completely disintegrated. The Winterpole pilots sat on their mounds of earth in the ocean and cried for help.

Rick pulled Evie to her feet. "We should get off this boat," he said, and then, as if to reinforce his point, his foot broke through a patch of the deck, which had turned to sand.

They ran to the edge of the boat, which continued to break apart beneath them.

"We have to get back to the *Roost*," Evie said.

"Do you think that's safe?" Rick asked, looking to her for advice. "I'm worried the *Roost* will break apart like the rest of the hoverships."

Evie smiled. "Don't forget. The *Roost* is a tree. It's already organic matter, so the Eden Compound won't convert it."

"Good point," Rick said. "And lucky for us, that glue net is anything but organic."

Sure enough, the blue sticky net that had anchored the *Roost* transformed into fresh water before their eyes and trickled away. Unfortunately, their hovership was still a good distance from the yacht. Evie didn't know how they were going to get over there to safety.

"Perhaps I can be of assistance," 2-Tor said from behind them.

Evie had forgotten about 2-Tor! Her heart sank at the thought of her robot guardian. What had the Eden Compound done to his metal body? She was afraid to look.

But she did. The bright green fluid shimmered on his chest plate. He tilted his beak to the sky and cawed. The Eden Compound put little speckled bumps on every inch of him.

Rick ran to the robot in a frivolous attempt to shield him from the rain. "2-Tor! We have to get you to safety."

"Do not fret, children. It is all right." The speckles sprouted. Wet, black feathers emerged like ferns after a rainstorm. His camera eyes turned the glossy yellow of a real crow. His beak changed color. The silver feathers of his wings followed suit. In a few seconds, all of 2-Tor had ceased to be robotic and had become real crow! Only the cracked television screen remained.

"Flying feathers! 2-Tor, you're real! You're a real bird." Evie jumped up and down like her shoes were made of super-bouncy balls.

2-Tor squawked, "I say! This is quite stimulating. I'm hungry! I have never been hungry before."

Rick grabbed 2-Tor by his soft feathered wing. "We have sandwiches back on the *Roost*. We should go there now!"

With a quick swipe, 2-Tor snatched the children with his talons and flapped his massive black wings. He blasted into the air on a direct course with the *Roost*, just as the yacht broke apart and everyone on board tumbled into the sea.

In seconds, 2-Tor, Evie, and Rick were aboard their beloved hovership and in the sky.

They flew high above the mayhem. Evie watched out the window as all her dreams came true. Off on the horizon, the rainstorm continued. All the floating garbage converged, forming the rich, natural foundation of her new world. A jewel in the middle of the Pacific. An endless field of rolling green, with rocky outcroppings and white beaches at the shoreline. Evie smiled.

It was her triumph. It was hope for the future. It was the eighth continent.

31

THOSE STUPID, UGLY LANES, VESUVIA THOUGHT AS SHE FLOATED ALONE IN THE MIDDLE OF THE OCEAN.

This is all their fault.

She clung to a floating bag of trash, one of the few to survive the apocalyptic use of the Eden Compound. Vesuvia hated garbage, would not be caught dead near garbage, but unfortunately for her, she hated drowning more, and so she clung like a rat to driftwood. Disgusting. Disgusting.

Her plastic clothes had been completely destroyed by the Eden Compound. Her skin was smeared with dirt, but she retained the slightest bit of modesty thanks to a few soggy green leaves that she wore like a bikini. She tried to look at the bright side. At least she was still better dressed than Evie Lane.

She had hit her head as she fell from her crumbling yacht, got knocked out, and woke up hugging this stinky garbage ball, without another soul as far as she could see. She must have floated clear of the garbage patch and gotten lost. She did not know what had happened to the rest of her fleet or to the Winterpole agents. People were going to pay through their eyeballs for all the money she had lost on this operation. Countless people were missing, but who cared about them? Her fleet was gone. Her beautiful pink fleet.

She did have an idea of what happened to the Lane kids. They had escaped in their tacky hovership with their tacky robot bird and gotten the tacky continent they wanted. She had already thought of twelve ways to steal the eighth continent away from them so that she could make New Miami.

DOOOOOOOOOOOOOOOOT!

Vesuvia looked in the direction of the sound. A speck had appeared on the horizon. She squinted, but it was too hard to see.

Minutes passed, and the speck grew into a boat. She recognized it as one of Winterpole's search-and-rescue vessels.

"Over here! Hey! Heeeeey! Help! Pleeease heeeeeeeeelp!!!!" Vesuvia clung to the trash bag with one hand and waved with the other. It was a rescue boat. She was saved!

The boat pulled up in front of her stinky flotation device.

Barry and Larry peered down at her from the deck of the ship. "Well, hey!" Barry said. "It's a girl. What are you doing hanging around out here, miss?"

Someone pushed them aside and glanced down in the water at Vesuvia. *Diana!* Thank good gracious relief. She really was saved.

But then Diana pointed at Vesuvia and said, "That's her, the super-secret CEO of Condo Corp."

Barry and Larry grabbed a giant fishing net and scooped

Vesuvia out of the water. They dumped her on the deck, where the trash bag broke, covering her in soggy coffee grounds and moldy lettuce.

Mister Snow appeared from inside the ship's cabin. "Oh, good. You found her. Hello, again, Miss Piffle. Your friend Miss Maple informed me of your impressive status as Condo Corp's CEO."

That wretched traitor! Diana had sold her out. She would add that girl to the ISES hate list the first chance she got. At the moment, Vesuvia had bigger fish to fool.

Widening and watering her eyes as best she could, Vesuvia gave Mister Snow her best impression of a little lost bunny. "I don't know what you mean, sir. You must have me confused with my father. He is the CEO of Condo Corp."

"Nice try," Mister Snow said. "But Diana told us everything, about how you are secretly running the corporation. We wondered how someone as clumsy as Donald Piffle could be so diabolical. We should have realized someone else was pulling the strings. I suppose you are aware that Condo Corp is the all-time largest violator of Winterpole statutes in history."

"It's not my fault your stupid statutes don't have a provision for double-decker oceans!" Vesuvia snapped.

Mister Snow nodded to Diana. "Mm. You're right. She does have a temper."

"I told you," Diana said quietly.

Turning back to Vesuvia, Mister Snow said, "Don't worry, my dear. You are still young. I promise, with good behavior, you'll be out of the Prison at the Pole in time for your eightieth birthday."

"My what?! You can't do that!"

Mister Snow raised his eyebrows. "Winterpole Statute UH-33: contradicting a Winterpole officer. That should make it your eighty-first birthday."

Vesuvia roared, and Diana made the strangest face. It was a bizarre contortion that Vesuvia had never seen her ex–best friend make before, this kind of upturn at the sides of her mouth, and a raising of her cheeks.

Then she realized. Diana was smiling.

32

AN UNTOUCHED CONTINENT LAY BEFORE THEM, A BOUNDLESS LAND OF LIFE AND OPPORTUNITY.

Like a blank canvas, the eighth continent begged for Rick and Evie to use their creativity to paint upon it the world they desired.

It had been six weeks since what the news had begun to call the Battle of the Garbage Patch, when the Eden Compound had transformed the Texas-sized mound of trash into the land where they now stood. Thus far, the new landscape had no name, but Rick had already begun to call it home.

After the *Roost* had rendezvoused with the *Drongo*, they had first spent time with their parents, telling them the tale of their adventures. 2-Tor never stopped apologizing. Apparently he had been quiet about the fact that he held himself responsible for all the danger they had faced. No one blamed the giant talking crow. Rick couldn't reprogram the birdbot anymore, so he gave him a big plate of worms as a thank-you present for taking care of them on their trip.

2-Tor said they were the best thing he'd ever tasted.

"They're the only thing you've ever tasted," Rick said.

In all honesty, Mom *was* pretty mad about the whole thing. They had disobeyed her and had risked their dad's freedom and their own, all for a chance at the eighth continent. But even Mom couldn't argue with the results, and she admired their motives. Rick still smiled when he thought of the hug he and Evie got from her when they were reunited.

"I was so worried about you! My brave, crazy little children." It was nice to see Mom and Evie make up. Mom could see that Evie had set her mind on a goal and had accomplished something truly great.

Dad was as happy as he had been that time they visited the Kuala Lumpur Bird Park. Once he was free of the squid-cuff, he draped himself in electronics and danced on the fields of the new continent. "FREEDOM!" he cheered at random moments . . . like whenever he was running on the beach or brushing his teeth.

Rick took a break from video games. "The eighth continent is cooler than any game. Think of everything we can do! We have to start building. We need trees, and roads, and houses—tree houses, of course. We can build laboratories, and a school, a town hall, anything we want!"

But the truth was, Rick didn't need all that. All he needed he already had: his parents, his sister, a new pet tiger cat, and the continent. From there he could start cleaning up the rest of the world. The Eden Compound was gone, but there was still a lot of garbage out there making the planet sick. He would need to come up with new ways to solve that problem. It was something to be proud of, a mission for Lane Industries, his father, and himself.

On a small hilltop on the south side of the continent, overlooking the ocean, they built a stone marker as a remembrance of their friend Doctor Evan Grant. Niels Bohr sunned himself on the hilltop every day, until the afternoon, when Rick and Evie would come with their parents to pay their respects, and the tiger cat would follow them back to the beach for supper.

At the edge of the continent, Rick sat around a fire with his family, the first settlers of this new world. There would be a lot of work, and many more adventures, but for the moment, Rick was happy to relax, enjoy his success, and imagine the possibilities.

"Hey, what's that?" Evie asked as she blew on the flaming marshmallow she was holding on a stick.

Rick followed her gaze. Near the horizon, silhouetted by the setting sun behind them, a number of shadowy shapes moved across the water, toward the continent. "What is that?"

Dad put down his guitar and rose from his lawn chair. "I could fire up the *Roost*, check it out."

"No . . ." Rick said. "I think I can see it. It's . . . they're . . . animals."

Dozens of them moved across the water, birds and eels and ferrets and grizzly bears, flying and slithering and swimming toward the continent. And in the middle of the pack, a giant bullet-shaped shark. Rick could see that even though his family had just created the eighth continent, someone was already trying to take it away, and Rick knew who.

For the animals were made of plastic.

And they were pink.

MATT LONDON (http://themattlondon.com) is a writer, video game designer, and avid recycler who has published short fiction and articles about movies, TV, video games, and other nerdy stuff. Matt is a graduate of The Clarion Writers Workshop, and studied computers, cameras, rockets, and robots at New York University. When not investigating lost civilizations, Matt explores the mysterious island where he lives — Manhattan.

Find out more at
8THCONTINENTBOOKS.COM